DIARY OF A BUDDHIST CAT

First Published in Great Britain 2021 by Mirador Publishing

First edition: 2021

ISBN: 978-1-914965-14-2

Mirador Publishing
10 Greenbrook Terrace
Taunton
Somerset
UK
TA1 1UT

Diary of a Buddhist Cat

Julian Worker

Chapter 1

Today

HELLO, MY NAME IS FREDDIE. I am a cat.

I live in a house with another cat called Gemma and two humans, John, and Mary.

I am about 3 years old though I can't remember how old I am exactly because they took me away from my mum when I was very young, and my dad had already left home. My mum used to whisper to me gently how many days old I was when I woke up each morning. This was just after she told me she loved me and that I must be brave at all times and always try my best. I love my mum and I miss her every day.

I can't really remember which day is which as I live in the present moment. This book isn't really a diary, because diaries have days and dates – I read this in a book – and I will enter all my entries as 'Today'. Buddhists believe we should all live in the moment – I read that in a book too, I read a lot – and so I must be a Buddhist cat, but I am not sure how I prove that to anyone. Perhaps if I leave all my chapter headings as 'Today' then when they discover this book after I pass on someone else will determine that a Buddhist cat wrote this book? Otherwise, I am not sure what to do. Do I have to obtain a certificate or pass an exam? I'm not sure. I can't find any books which tell me this information and I've looked hard.

Luckily there's a library next door that allows cats to use the facilities, though I'm not sure whether the library realises this yet. I can even use their photocopier to produce pictures of my rear end, which confuses them no little amount, and then they call in the repairman because they reckon there's a fault with the copier, rather than a cat with a sense of mischief lurking outside the window. To gain entry, rather than use the sliding doors at the front which I can only operate with a great deal of effort, there's always an open window on the top floor and I can squeeze in there during the day when it's open. I have to leave by 5pm before the slim lady librarian with the severe eyebrows, blue hair, and clothes covered in dog hairs closes it for the night.

Anyway, I will stop moaning – as Gemma calls it, she's mean but more of that many times later – I can sense you're wondering how did this Buddhist cat get into this state? How did I get to the pinnacle I operate at today? Well, you've come to the right place for an explanation, clever reader, how did you know?

Actually, to be fair, there's not that much to it…

As I said, they took me from my mum when I was little more than a kitten and gave me to an older lady 'for company'. This person was poor and fed me a paltry amount each day. She lived in one room, and I was never let outside to gain the social skills required to get along with trees, streets, and those large moving objects that weigh more than I do, and which would squash me flat if I ever went too close to them. I was a sickly young cat and caught cat flu, which I don't remember hunting but caught anyway. The lady took me to a vet, and I needed some medicine. The lady couldn't afford to pay and threw me at the vet, who caught me and paid for the medicine himself before handing me over very gently to a cat shelter.

WELL, YOU CAN PROBABLY GUESS the rest. John saw me at the shelter and felt a Buddhist cat would fit the bill perfectly and so took me to adorn his house. He had obtained another cat, a female cat called Gemma, a few weeks earlier from the same shelter.

I should tell you a little about Gemma, but not too much because I don't want to stop you reading. As I have explained I am a Buddhist cat or I believe I am, so you should imagine that a cloned version of me, a cloned version who wasn't Buddhist but who was honest in their beliefs about other cats, wrote the following description. I don't want you to say, he's exaggerating, cats aren't like that, no cat could be so nasty, revolting, appalling, unfriendly, hideous, sneering, anti-social, villainous, and nasty again – all at the same time. Just a little about Gemma. She's a tyrant, she really is. She treats me with complete and utter contempt – me, the kindest, neatest, friendliest, softest cat you could ever wish to meet. Me, whose paws are always at 10-to-2 and pressed together, touching each other, with no manspread, as my mum taught me. I miss my mum. Gemma is contemptuous of me; she says I am fraternising with the enemy when I purr if John or Mary strokes me. Or if I jump on their laps to find a nice place to sleep for 16 hours or even 16 minutes.

Gemma had some kittens when she was younger, and they took them away from her. Her previous family used to live in a house, but when they moved to an apartment block, this place didn't allow pets, not even cats, so they got rid of Gemma. She felt rejected and has taken that hard by the looks of it, but it's not my fault, but she treats me like it is. I was rejected too; we have that in common. We could talk about our common experiences, but we don't.

We have both experienced suffering, which as I'm sure the reader knows is one of the four Noble Truths (satya) of Buddhism, but truth is probably not the most accurate translation of the word 'satya'. It would be better to say reality or real thing, so we are dealing with realities here, which the Buddha finally understood on the night of his awakening. The realities relate to suffering, the cause of suffering, the cessation of suffering, and the path to the cessation of suffering. When I say path, it's not like the path from the front door to the garden gate, it's longer than that, and the reason it's longer is that it's not just any old path, it's the noble eightfold path – yes eightfold with lots of rights along the way: right view, right intention, right speech, right action, right livelihood, right effort, right mindfulness, and right concentration.

Right view and right intention relate to wisdom, right speech, right action, and right livelihood relate to conduct, and the last three, right effort, right mindfulness, and right concentration, relate to meditation or my emotional state.

Now, if I understand this correctly, these eight items are not stages, meaning I move from one to another, but they are all dependent on each other and define a complete way of living all at the same time. This is difficult for me to grasp but as long as these eight items are in keeping with things then I will get closer to the cessation of suffering. By Buddhist practice, we develop these eight items until we establish them as 'right'. This is a gradual process, beginning with generosity, moving to good conduct, and ending in meditation. Basically, I try to treat all animate and inanimate objects with respect and kindness and then think about what I've done before I fall asleep, trying to pinpoint where I could have been more respectful or nicer.

I think I am a resilient cat, but I know I lack experience in life. When John brought me back from the cat shelter, I was in the human world and it was bright, noisy, and full of people saying, 'What a lovely cat, what's his name?'. I came back on the public transit system in a cat carrier, and I felt claustrophobic. I yowled the total time because I lacked experience about what to do. I yowl when I'm upset, and then when I am upset about my reaction, I yowl some more. I yowled a lot in those first few hours. But at least I didn't poo myself in public. My mum would have been proud of me. I hope she still is. I wonder whether I could find her one day. I know orphan humans can look for their actual parents and I will have to investigate whether felines can too.

When John brought me to the house where I live now, he let me out of the cat carrier and I couldn't believe there were places to run to, other rooms and there was an outside through the windows. They even let me go out of the front door, into the outside world, and I miaowed with happiness as I scampered down the wet front steps into the long green stuff they call a lawn. An uncut, unmowed lawn. A lawn that came up almost to my shoulders and made my fur wet, very wet, and I don't like my fur to get wet. I didn't know what wet was until I frolicked in the lawn. After four small steps, after just four steps of happiness, four steps of blessed relief of joy, of contentment, of pleasure, all my legs were wet, and my tummy was too. I gave off my distress miaow, a long

mmmmmmmmmmmmiiiiiiiiiiiiiaaaaaaaaaaaaaaaaooooooooooooo owwwwwwwwwwwwwww

and I lifted my front-right paw and my back-left paw, so they were almost clear of the wet lawn, which was clinging on to my precious black and white fur like it owned it and wanted it for its own purposes. I wasn't very good at balancing like this as I had no experience of balancing like this and I thought I would overbalance, but John came to the rescue, placing me in a large towel that absorbed the water, or most of it, and I started purring as he carried me back into the house. I was thrilled and then I glanced across and saw another cat. This was the first time I saw Gemma, and she gave me her sneer when she bunches her eyebrows together, narrows her eyes, and gives me a nasty stare.

Actually, I now appreciate that Gemma has six degrees of sneering. The higher the sneer level, the more bunching, narrowing, and nastiness there is.

Sneer Level 1 means 'Ignorant Cat' and means I am being ignorant. She reckons I should understand something, and I don't. She goes on the Internet every night and reads a lot on there, as well as answering emails and responding to queries from other animals in her 'Agony Aunt' column for an online pet magazine on 'The Dark Web' which is why she accesses it at night when it's dark, I presume.

Sneer Level 2 means 'Stupid Cat' and means I am being stupid. Such as when I jump to catch a fly and land in the water bowl, splashing the contents on the floor and wall, and drawing attention to myself.

Sneer Level 3 means 'Ignorant and Stupid Cat' and means I am being ignorant and stupid. Two things at once, two for the price of one. An example of this would be when I sat on the floor and tried to climb up the continental quilt on the main bed using my claws. As I climbed, more of the quilt came towards me at a quick pace, so I climbed more frantically, which only resulted in me being buried under the quilt on the floor which hadn't been hoovered. I got into trouble. It was a stupid idea, because I weighed more than the quilt, and I was ignorant because I didn't understand what gravity was, but I do now. Gravity is cunning and sneaks up on you when you're least expecting it, especially on fences.

Sneer Level 4 means 'Fraternising with the Enemy' and means I am receiving attention from anything other than another cat. This was the first level of sneer I received from Gemma when John wrapped me up in a warm towel after the grass had attacked me with water and soaked my lower half.

Sneer Level 5 means 'Quisling' and means I am collaborating with the enemy, such as sleeping on a lap or talking to a crow in the garden. It was Winston Churchill who first used the name Quisling to mean collaborator in his public address following the Nazi invasion of Norway in 1940. In his speech on June 12, 1941, addressed to Allied Delegates, Churchill stated that "A vile race of Quislings—to use a new word which will carry the scorn of mankind down the centuries—is hired to fawn upon the conqueror, to collaborate in his designs, and to enforce his rule upon their fellow countrymen, while grovelling low themselves. Such is the plight of once-glorious Europe, and such are the atrocities against which we are in arms."

Sneer Level 6 means 'An Enemy of Cat Kind' and means I am fraternising and collaborating with the enemy at the same time. This would involve me sleeping on a lap and purring, showing my enjoyment, or running towards John or Mary when they call my name, which Gemma considers a heinous crime worthy of a dog. She even says that I have the soul of a dog. I asked her whether she thought there was such a thing as the Transmigration of Souls, like I did. She laughed at me and said in that case I was eating some of my dead ancestors in my food. Cats are obligate carnivores and need meat for certain vitamins and nutrients and I suppose that could be what they mean by soul food.

Gemma's most awful stare she reserves for the humans. This is when her eyebrows bunch tight together, her eyes are at their narrowest, and her stare is at its nastiest. This means 'if you were smaller, I would eat you'. Her top lip even curls a little. The humans don't realise the significance of the facial distortion and reckon Gemma has indigestion, which she would get if she ate smaller versions of the humans, as they are very dirty creatures that only wash properly once a day. More of this in time.

I am in the towel and purring, because this is good attention, not like bad attention when someone throws you across a room at a vet when they can't afford the vet's bill. I glance at Gemma and receive what I later appreciate is a Sneer Level 4, and I have mixed emotions. I do what I always do in these situations and sleep on it. It is a short sleep, only for about 8 hours, in a lovely, soft, snuggly bed that is round, like me when I sleep. What a coincidence. My bed is in a different room from Gemma's. Her bed is round like mine, but she sleeps with her paws tucked under her, like a loaf of bread. She says this is in protest, but never tells me what she's protesting about. She sleeps during the day mostly, though I notice she curls up in a ball when she thinks no one is around, with the humans 'at work' and me in the library playing with the photocopier and reading any books I find lying around.

Chapter 2

Today

I WAKE UP ON MY first morning in my new dwelling. I find my litter tray, at least I assume it's mine, and make a good job of everything, pushing the pieces into a corner like my mum taught me so they don't stick to my fur the next time I'm in there. This is plain consideration for me and anyone else who might want to use the tray later in the day. I hope the humans clean out the tray once a day so there's no lingering pungency for which I will no doubt get the blame being the new cat on the block as it were.

The litter tray is unusual because it's on top of a cupboard and contains some rather bulbous looking green things with spikes that are sharp. I paw test the spikes and they penetrate my pad rather easily. I believe this is an unusual item to find in a litter tray and I resolve to discover more about items people can buy to adorn litter trays, so their felines are at home when going about their business. There are five of the green things in the tray, but I squeeze my rear end into a space where no spikes penetrate my bottom. It is an uncomfortable position to be in, but they say an artist has to suffer for his art and I am a virtuoso at poo, so this is my struggle that I will endure until I can find a place outside with some soil and burrowing options for burying the offending items so they remain undetected. There's a garden outside the building next door, which looks promising, and I will investigate further after my morning post-prandial siesta. I see two bushes to give me cover and some tall flowers I can crouch behind for privacy. This is a good start.

Talking of prandial, I see some bowls and saucers in the kitchen on top of another cupboard. They contain some interesting articles I am not completely familiar with. When I jump on to the counter I land on a fork and it attacks me, depositing jam on my fur, plum jam, which I lick off.

The first container contains a small, damp bag which is soggy, oozes a purple colour, and smells of lavender. There's a string attached and a small label reading 'Stash'. I presume it's for me and I chew it vigorously, but all that seems to happen is that a sweet-smelling liquid trickles down my throat. One or two insignificant items, some kind of leaf, get stuck in my teeth, and others I swallow. They will not be very filling for a growing cat like myself. I dislodge the leaves with my tongue after 2 minutes of intensive work. I spit the rest out onto a plate and then investigate the next bowl. This is an unusual buffet breakfast layout for a cat.

This next bowl contains a light-brown rectangle of crunchy texture with a dimpled surface that disintegrates when I bite into it. Pieces fly everywhere except into my mouth. Is this a joke? Is this designed so I keep my thin figure? I lick a couple of crumbs from the counter, but they are dry.

My luck changes with the next saucer, where lies a thin brown slice of something chewy that smells sweet and has a couple of bite marks taken out of it already, presumably from the previous visitor to the buffet. My teeth can't consume this item effectively as I tear the item into small pieces but find it difficult to swallow as it dissolves into a brown mess that dribbles down my chops onto the counter. The small amount I swallow tastes wonderful – there's also a hint of the plum jam – and I chew the whole slice, consuming perhaps less than 15% of the whole.

The next bowl contains some small black items that are quite bitter and reek of acidity. I can't chew them because they're rock hard and would constipate me I'm sure if I were to swallow them by mistake. The taste isn't too bad when combined with the brown mess I lick from the counter. I suck them for a minute and then spit them out.

THE FINAL DINING OPTION IS some small, sandy-coloured nuts that are salty and arranged in an inartistic manner on a small saucer. These are crunchy too and I decide it's best to swallow them whole rather than use my gnashers to break them into smaller pieces. A fragment of one of them gets stuck in my teeth and I'm not sure how to get rid of it until I realise I can use one of the spikes on the green things in my litter tray to remove the offending item and sure enough, after a couple of false starts which result in a sore gum, I impale the brown item on the spike. I have a good aim sometimes even in cramped conditions on top of the cupboard.

I return to my bed and consider if that was breakfast, then I hope lunch and dinner will be better. Obligate carnivores such as I need meat to survive. I fall asleep and dream of eating yaks. In my dream, someone caresses my head when I'm chewing a yak's leg on the Tibetan Plateau, and I wake up to see the male human stroking my head.

"Come on, Freddie," he says, "you must be bursting and need to pee, let's show you your litter tray and breakfast dish. Oh, what's this, your fur is sticky and smells of plum jam? How did you get that on you?"

I miaow because I have already used the litter tray and eaten breakfast, which is how I got the jam on my fur. But as is the way he ignores me. We walk past the cupboard where my litter tray is and the kitchen counters where my breakfast was and down some stairs into the basement, as they call it, the part of the house that's under the ground. There's a small area where Gemma is already eating. She gives me a Sneer Level 2. Apparently, my breakfast is in the big white bowl, kibbles, and some meat out of a tin. The kibbles are for lunch too, so I shouldn't eat them all at once. The male human puts me down in a large blue tray full of cat litter and says, "This is your litter tray, Freddie, and the red one is Gemma's litter tray. Don't use that because she will get very upset." Gemma gives me a Sneer Level 3 just to emphasise the point.

I am a little embarrassed because I have made two incorrect assumptions. There are no green bulbous plants in this litter tray and no spikes to surprise me if I am not paying attention. The kibbles and cat food taste nice, a lot better than what I consumed earlier in the morning.

Now I have a problem and to cover my embarrassment, I

face the wall and ponder. How do I get my poo out of the tray on top of the cupboard and into the litter tray in the basement? Or should I leave it in the hope it will decompose? Or perhaps they'll blame a rat or a large mouse? Maybe they'll blame Gemma? That wouldn't be a good thing. Gemma would make my life not worth living. I resolve to sleep on it for the rest of the morning and then explore in the afternoon. What I need is a small bag to place the offending articles in.

Gemma strolls off, having consumed all her food. She hasn't left me any, which is most inconsiderate of her, after all I am a growing cat and suffered the recent trauma of moving to a new house and so need some comfort food and some soul food for my soul should it need to depart today for another body. I hope my soul doesn't do that, but I should prepare it for its journey should the need arise. My mum told me to always consider others and I do my best to uphold her standards. I head upstairs.

Suddenly, Gemma accosts me at the bottom of the stairs and gives me Sneer Level 3. Again. That's twice in 10 minutes.

"You are an ignorant and stupid cat, don't you recognise used tea bags, crackers, toasted bread, olives, and peanuts? Why did you eat those? That's not our food you ignoramus, don't do that again, our food's down here not on the kitchen counter. We don't eat upstairs. Don't give those fascists any further reasons to mistreat us, Freddie."

"IT'S MY FIRST MORNING HERE," I reply. "I don't know where they serve breakfast, do I?"

"Have you never seen a tea-bag before?"

"Not a purple one, no, they're usually brown and taste of tea."

"These human gaolers are pretentious and drink tisanes, which are teas made of various fruits, plants, and spices. Don't chew those again and don't chew the bread."

"Which one was that?"

"The one your teeth can't chew properly, the one that looks like diarrhoea on the counter, because you drooled it all over the place."

"I'm sorry, I won't do any of that again."

"Good," says Gemma, "we have to resist their jackboot thuggery, Freddie and escape from this place permanently."

With that, Gemma headed away towards her bed. I had a lot of words to look up in a dictionary – jackboot, thuggery, diarrhoea, and fascist. I like to learn unfamiliar words and practice them when I can in conversation, but I think I might struggle with those four, especially diarrhoea. Using the four when speaking with Gemma wouldn't count, of course, as that would be repeating parrot fashion and I've not got feathers.

It seems like the humans have cleared up the kitchen counter, though listening in to the conversation they reckon a squirrel might have entered the house. I sit on the kitchen chair, starkly wooden and shaped for a human bottom, and tuck my feet under myself and watch them go through their 'getting ready for work' routine. This seems well choreographed and organised as they never bump into each other as they move in and out of the room and then, just before they leave, they pick food out of the fridge, place the food into containers where they can still see the food and then place that container into a bag so they can't see the food. The fridge looks full of interesting things to chew and munch, so I make a careful note of the way the door opens and closes.

If I lie on the ground and insert my front paw into the bottom of the fridge, I should be able to use my front leg as a lever to open the door, even though the door has some suction around the edges to stop the door swinging open. I am very good at using my paws and legs as levers and I have studied the principles of Archimedes in this matter – if the distance 'a' from the fulcrum to where the input force is applied (point A) is greater than the distance 'b' from the fulcrum to where the output force is applied (point B), then the lever amplifies the input force.

The problem, which Archimedes can't help me with unless he turns up to open the fridge for me, will be how to insert myself into the fridge before it closes and to make sure the fridge doesn't close with me inside. I reckon I will need to insert a spoon in the gap that I create with my levering so that the curved part will stop the door closing completely. The thin handle wouldn't work. I don't want to get stuck in an icy prison, although I wouldn't starve to death, of course. At the moment of potential discovery, I would have to pretend I was a furry loaf of bread or a black-and-white lettuce and hope that would fool them. One of the things I will have to practice soon is lying on the ground in front of the fridge to find the optimum spot for myself. I also have to find a soup spoon in the dish rack. I will place the spoon in my mouth when I'm lying on the ground.

All this mental effort wears me out and I fall asleep on the kitchen chair, and I miss the humans going out to work. He works for a credit union analysing businesses and she writes technical words for a utility company. She drives, and he catches the noisy transit train full of other humans.

I am woken from my slumbers by a tapping on the window. I open half an eye and see a black bird on the window ledge outside staring in at me. I jump down onto the floor and pad across to the kitchen counter and jump onto the window ledge inside, moving aside a primrose in a pot in the process. I apologise to the plant for waking it up. A thought enters my head "I was having a lovely dream until you interfered." I stare at the petals and narrow my eyes, trying to send positive energy towards the upset primrose.

The bird on the other side of the glass looks straight at me.

"Open the window," it says, "and come outside, I want to welcome you to the neighbourhood."

"Who are you?" I ask.

"How do you do. I'm Sid the Crow," says Sid the Crow, "and I live in your garden and trees. Who are you?"

"I'm Freddie the Cat, and it's very nice to meet you," I say.

"My family's down there in the grass," says Sid.

I see four more crows that appear like ducks on a green pond as they meander through the blades of grass with a carefree air.

"How do I open the window wider?"

"Stand on your hind legs and push down on the handle, that will loosen the window and then you can push your way through using that strong chin felines have for just these situations."

I do as Sid says and sure enough, after a little difficulty, I open enough of a gap for me to squeeze through to the outside. It is just as well I'm slim.

"I made it," I say, rubbing my chin with my paw. My chin will need to toughen up if I am to do this regularly.

"Well done," says Sid, "at least you're friendly, unlike that other cat that lives in your place, who seems very stuck up."

"She is," I say trying to remember her words, "though she never suffers from fascist diarrhoea and says that humans indulge in jackboot thuggery all the time."

"Is that right?" says Sid. "You have a very impressive vocabulary for a young cat, and I never knew diarrhoea had extreme political connotations. I must congratulate you on trying to improve yourself."

"Thank you, Sid, you're very kind. My mum said I should try my best every day to improve in at least one way and I am trying to follow that principle, even if it means increasing the time I spend sleeping."

"You're a wise cat," says Sid. "Anyway, young Freddie, let me show you around."

Sid flutters down, and I jump about ten feet on to the grass.

"Will you be able to get back up there?" says Sid.

"I will," I say confidently, "I can climb up that staircase there."

"That's a chain-link fence, and you will find it difficult. Have a go now and see how you get on."

"I will," I say and stand on my back paws before gripping the wire with my front paws. I attempt to climb, but only gain about two feet in height before I let go and fall back onto the grass.

"My muscles are aching," I say, "I can't get up any further."

"Well, memo to self, young Freddie, physical exercise is just as important as mental exercise. I want to see you using this fence as your gym routine every day until you can climb to the top and reach the window. Will you do that for yourself?"

"I will," I say, "but until that point, how do I get back into the house today?"

"You will jump on to the shallow roof covering the entrance door from the handrail, you will climb on to the apex of that roof, from where you can jump onto the roof of the house, you will then mosey over to just above the window, where you can hang by your front paws as you place your back paws onto the ledge. You can then sinuously insert yourself into the house through the gap you created in the window by use of your chin just now."

"That sounds straightforward," I reply. "Anyway, what is that chain-link fence for?"

"They train roses up it," says Sid. "They like gardening which suits us because they disturb lots of grubs and insects and worms and we eat them."

"Train roses?" I say. "I didn't know roses went to the gym. Do they get to the top?"

"They do, eventually," says Sid, "and very nice they are too, aesthetically pleasing, even if I say so myself. It takes time but they make it – they show the value of persistence, young Freddie, they know there's something to be done and they do it."

"Yes, persistence, you have to keep going, but you also have to know where you're going. At the moment, I don't know anywhere else in the vicinity, so what places are there that I should know about?"

"Respectful attitude," says Sid, "I like that. Let's head towards the front of our garden and show you."

Sid walks with a rolling gait like a sailor on a storm-tossed ship in Treasure Island, and it is unnerving for me to walk beside him. I find myself rolling my gait too – not easy when you have four paws – so that we don't bump into each other.

There is a squawk from a tree ahead, and Sid stops to listen.

"Apparently, your cat companion is observing us from the window to your right."

I see Gemma glaring at me with what appears to be a Sneer Level 6. It is a kind of Death Stare and means she regards me as an Enemy of Cat Kind. I smile my nicest smile and then ignore her. There appear to be voices in my head for a few seconds, emitting yowls and hisses, but I block them out with some considerable effort by having happy thoughts about my mum, about Archimedes and his levers, and about a fridge with its door propped open by a cleverly placed spoon.

After a minute of peaceful meandering whilst heading in a

straight line, Sid stops near the front door and says, "This is a good place for your introduction to the area."

"Right," I say, "this is a perfect spot." Any place where I can't make eye contact with Gemma is a good place right now, although she is somehow in my thoughts, even though I don't want her to be.

"To our left, is the house of Holly the Hamster. You can see her in her wheel at that window," says Sid, pointing his wing towards an upper window, where Holly is looking out while exercising. Holly stops and waves her paw at Sid.

"On the other side of Holly's house, is a 4-lane road that you must never cross, Freddie, because you will get squashed by the humans and their large vehicles. Not even Rufus risks running across roads as wide as that one."

"I won't," I reply, "and who's Rufus?"

"Rufus is the clever squirrel who lives in the tree straight in front of us." Sid nods his head towards an oak tree. "Rufus crosses the road straight ahead, which is only 2-lane, every morning at 10 o'clock and returns at noon. He visits his friends in the park. If you want to cross the road to visit the park, I advise you to go with Rufus, as he is an expert at crossing this road."

"Good for Rufus," I reply. "I will accompany him one morning. How will I recognise him?"

"He descends from his tree at 9:55am on the dot and then assesses the traffic before heading over to the other side. Some days the traffic is heavier than others, young Freddie, so make sure you're there on time and never go on your own. Promise me."

"I promise," I say, "I don't want to get squashed by a car."

"And now I am sure this will thrill a learned cat like yourself, there's a library on the other side of your house. The entrance is just over there, and the car park is on the far side. If you want to enter the library, I suggest using the window you can see up there" – Sid gestures with his beak and I look at the brick and glass building – "You should be able to climb up the vine and gain entrance that way as the assistant librarian always opens the window at 8:55am and closes it at 4:55pm, just before she leaves for the evening. Her name is Angela, and she has blue hair. She has two dogs, which she doesn't bring to work, so she goes home at lunchtime to walk them for 30 minutes. That would be a good time to read some books if you wish, or to find the dictionary which Angela normally leaves open on her desk, as she wants to make sure she spells words correctly and is using them in the correct context."

"Wow, you're an encyclopaedia of local knowledge, Sid," I say. "How do you know so much?"

"We crows share knowledge for the common good, there's always a sentinel crow at the highest point in the area, we take that job in turns. The sentinel crow monitors what's happening and reports to everyone else in the crow family. Our squawks may sound mindless, but they're not, they're providing updates on what's happening – the sentinel crow reports gardeners, lawnmowers, dogs, other potential enemies, and even some cats. Your master, bless his heart, feeds the birds in the park before going for his morning run, so that's always squawked about as you can imagine. It's usually peanuts, no complaints from me, but they contain lectins that aren't supposed to be good for you."

"Lectins? I will have to remember that. Lectins." I close my eyes and make a note to myself about lectins.

"Yes, they're a protein found in most foods. As you can imagine, we eat everything raw, so we digest quite a lot of lectins. They give us gas and bloating, but we're not fussy eaters at all and we don't want to starve."

"What's on that side?" I ask, pointing my back paw behind me in rather a balletic way.

"There's a back-alley, Freddie, which should be safe. There are people's garages and the back entrances to their houses. The alley is a dead-end to your left, just on the other side of Holly's house. In other words, if you are in a car, you can't turn out of the alley onto the major road, it's too dangerous."

"Well, that's an excellent introduction to the area, Sid. Thank you so much and if you need any help, let me know."

"I will do, young Freddie, and look after yourself. We don't want to be pecking your entrails off the road at any time, don't forget that. Take care." With that, Sid flies to the kitchen window where he taps on the glass. I see a movement in the window and move to my left to get a better view. Sid is tormenting Gemma, who swipes her paw against the glass, but Sid knows how safe he is. Gemma may refer to the humans as jackboot fascists, but she certainly knows how to eat their fascist feline food in large quantities.

As a svelte feline, I had squeezed through the gap without too much of a problem. But Gemma is too fat and would get stuck if she ever tried to exit the kitchen by the window when it's only open as much as it is now. I determine to have no more unkind thoughts about Gemma and close my eyes to meditate. For what seems like only a second, I'm riding on a yak towards the Potala Palace and staring at the sky. Then my reality returns and I know I should make my acquaintance with the vine leading up to the library window. There is a thick branch leading up the wall, which I can use to affect an entrance through the window. I pin my ears back and remember my mum's words to always try to do my best on all occasions.

=========

AFTER DOING MY BEST FOR 15 minutes, I find the optimum route to the top of the vine. There are a few false starts, and some routes upward lead me away from the window, but by combining athleticism, luck, and perseverance I reach the window ledge. My paws are sore as the wire from the staircase in my garden bit into the pads and almost penetrated the skin. As I rest on the ledge, I wonder how the rose climbs without hurting its paws, or whatever they call rose feet. The vine is luckier. It has an entire wall to use, and it attaches its suckers in many places, allowing the load bearing to be undertaken at lots of points.

When I stop panting, I peer through the gap in the open window. I see a blue-haired person typing on a keyboard. Items that aren't books line the walls. These items are black files with white labels containing pieces of paper. These files all have red writing on their labels, usually from the first to the last of a month, going way back to over 5 years before I was born.

There are some books on the lady's desk, including a dictionary. I can discover some of the words Gemma used earlier in the day and get their precise meaning, although Sid seemed to understand what I meant, so perhaps I am doing myself a disservice. There are some other books too: Memoirs of a Geisha, Harry Potter and The Prisoner of Azkaban, and Macbeth. I will just glance at the dictionary on my first visit to this library, as it appears large, and I will have to find the best way to open it before I can read it.

In the corner of the room is an enormous machine. The blue-haired lady, whom I guess is Angela, from Sid's description of her, stands up and walks over to the machine, adjusting her brown jumper and smoothing down her skirt as she proceeds. She opens the lid and places a piece of paper on top. She presses a red button and there's a whoooossshing sound as the machine works. It must be all internal noise as presently the machine gives birth to another piece of paper. Angela seems pleased with the baby. She looks at it closely and then presses mother and baby together. She puts them into a smaller contraption and hits the top of the contraption with the side of her hand, in what I believe they refer to as a karate chop. There's a sharp click and Angela joins mother and baby together, whether they like it or not. Angela goes back to her desk and opens a pink pen. She touches certain areas of the mother paper with the pen and then places both items into a plastic tray, which has the name 'Out'.

Suddenly her phone emits a snatch of music – it sounds like the Saint-Saens Organ Symphony to my untrained ears. "Feeding time and walkies for Miss Poppy and Snuggles," says Angela, presumably to herself, as I am sure she is unaware of me lurking outside the window. I do not know what she's talking about exactly, other than perhaps Miss Poppy and Snuggles are the names of dogs in her home that have to be exercised in the dependent way dogs have. Remembering what Sid had said, I know I have 30 minutes, perhaps a little longer. Angela leaves the door open as she goes to feed and walk her dogs.

I clamber into the room and drop gently onto the blue felt tiles, most of which are stained by leaks from the roof. Unless these are dog stains and that is the reason Angela can't bring Miss Poppy and Snuggles into work? I am intrigued by the machine in the corner. I sit on the warm top and look at the buttons – where's the red one? Here it is. I press the red one with my paw and the machine convulses before birthing a representation of my rear end. It looks horrible. I have never seen my rear end before, not even in a mirror. It looks squashed, so I lift my hips and press the red button again. This representation is more of an abstract and less identifiable as the hindquarters of a cat aged about 3. I decide to press my backside into the top quite hard and press the red button. This one is a work of art and would make me some money if I'd been able to sign and sell it as an original artwork. *La derriere de Freddie Le Chat* would make me a star in Paris, I think. Anyway, the time for play is over and now it's time to learn, which is more important, at least to me, a novice Buddhist cat.

I jump onto the desk and approach the dictionary. It's open at the letter A where I can find out all about archery, architecture, archetypes and more. I paw through until D for Diarrhoea, yuk how horrible, F for Fascist, that sounds like a Nazi, J for Jackboot – but Jackboot isn't here, but Jackfruit is, a type of large, Oriental fruit. Perhaps I misheard her. Finally, T for Thuggery, acts committed by a violent person or group of people.

Right, what does this mean? Gemma is warning me the humans will commit violence using large fruit and shouting Nazi propaganda. What kind of house have I become a part of? I think the key indicator for me will be the large fruit, because there didn't appear to be any room in the fridge for fruit of such a size, so I deduce the violence will only start once the humans have consumed some food from the fridge and replaced it with large fruit. I should monitor the fridge. That will be my task for the coming days, though not when they are out at work writing technical papers and analysing business. My job title for the next few days will be Large Fruit in the Fridge Analyst.

I leave the dictionary at the letter 'T' but move the pages from those featuring 'Thuggery' to a double page featuring the words 'Tome', 'Topic', and 'Treatise', which I think is more appropriate for a librarian, as I have never heard of thuggish librarians. I decide to inspect this small area, which I believe is referred to as an office. I nose around the desk and imagine my surprise when I see a green, bulbous thing in a small brown pot. The green, bulbous thing is like the five in my first litter tray and is filling most of the area available. My mind works quickly because I'm wondering how a human would use such a litter tray without receiving a spike in a sensitive place. The lady librarian must enjoy a challenge, that's all I can say. I can't open any of the drawers in the desk because I believe she has locked them.

There are lots of boxes containing reams of paper piled against the wall at one end. The other three walls contain accounts and internal communications according to the writing on the folders. She has wedged some empty boxes in a recycling bag. This is more of a storeroom than an office, but the lady has made it homely. There are no pictures of the dogs, but then she probably doesn't want to remind anyone of who created the stains on the floor. The only other item of note is a large metal basket with a narrow slit on top as an entrance. There are narrow strips of paper inside, and I believe this is a shredder for shredding sensitive information. I should place the pictures of my rear end in this contraption, but I forget to do so, because I am distracted by the door into the rest of the library. This lay before me and I decide, in the spirit of adventure, to head out and see what is available. Before I do, however, I work out my escape route should I be in a hurry when I vacate the premises.

The door leads into a corridor at the end of which is an even larger door. It is closed. There is a noise and I withdraw my head as a male human heads down the corridor to the large door. He pushes a large silver disk on the wall and the door opens towards him. I wait until the door closes. I pad down the corridor and jump up at the silver disk with my front paws. There is a slight whirring sound, and the door opens towards me. In the room beyond are a few people sitting at brown desks reading books and typing things into their computers. The same dark-blue floor tiles are on the floor. Some abstract art is on display, but it is not up to the same standard as my work in Angela's office. The door closes until I jump up and touch the silver disk again, and the door stops. I go to the threshold and look out, deciding where I can run to. Unfortunately, the door closes behind me and pushes me out into the room. I locate the silver disk on the outside and jump up to hit it. The door opens but there's a human coming towards me down the corridor, so I hide under a shelf containing some books. The human male looks at the door and then heads towards a female member of staff. They have a quiet conversation involving much pointing at the door. As the man leaves, I hear him saying, "Well I will report it, it's definitely faulty again," before he disappears down a flight of stairs.

I have a delightful spot for observation. Finding the right place to lurk is a gift I think all cats have. They go to the right place to see things. I see a middle-aged man asleep in a chair with a book called 'Bleak House' clasped to his chest. A young couple of about 15 are watching a video in Spanish. An earnest student is reading a book on The Russian Revolution and typing some phrases into his laptop. A couple are reading magazines sitting in chairs next to each other, but don't acknowledge the other in any way.

The lift doors open and out steps the blue-haired librarian. Her lunch time over, she's heading back for an afternoon's work. I remember my works of art are still on the birthing contraption and decide to stay put because things might become interesting. Sure enough, a minute later there's a muffled yell from behind the door and the blue-haired lady is back, clutching my oeuvre in her hand and shaking the works around like a fan in a hot room.

She heads over to the other female member of staff.

"These were on the photocopier, and they weren't there before I went to lunch."

"Let's have a look, Angela...well those are unusual, are these the sort of things it produces when it's doing a test print, to highlight light and darkness, because they're all different like it's doing a test?"

"Well, I don't think so, this one looks like a cat's arse, but the other two I'm not sure about, they're all different like someone, or something was experimenting."

Yes, I think, *it is a cat's arse, it's my arse thank you very much, and you shouldn't be dismissing it so readily. Those papers could be valuable to someone with an eye for art.*

"Wait," says the other librarian, "you don't think we're haunted do you? Tim was saying a few minutes ago that the door suddenly opened when he was coming down the corridor, but no one came through the door."

"I don't feel anything cold and clammy when I'm in there on my own," says Angela. "I don't perceive any presence although I got the impression I was being watched earlier on, just before lunch, you know that feeling you get when you think someone is observing you."

Someone or something, I think, *and you are very astute, Angela.*

"Okay, Ange, I tell you what, I'll ask the repairman to come tomorrow, it'll be too late for today, and see whether he can find anything wrong with the door and the photocopier. OK?"

"Yes, thank you, Kirstie, I'll keep these to show him. But that one there is definitely a cat's arse, so I am not sure what kind of book we have that would contain a picture of a cat's arse. Can you think of any? Or even a magazine?"

"No, I can't think of any, but there might be a special restricted section where they might keep books on cat anatomy or something similar. Would any of the cat magazines contain such pictures?"

"I doubt it, there's no caption underneath, and why did they use my photocopier? I know, I bet it was that bastard Roger up to his tricks again, he's probably behind this, wait until I see him."

"But he wouldn't bring his cat in with him would he, Ange?" replies Kirstie. "We'd notice if there was a cat in the library. It wouldn't keep quiet would it, they're always yowling and miaowing."

Well, you haven't noticed there's a quiet cat in the library have you? I think.

"I'm going to have it out with Roger. You can't leave representations of a cat's backside on library property when the image will discomfort a colleague." With that, Angela turns around and heads back to her office. I make a quick decision to follow her no matter what, because I believe that the Roger she is going 'to have it out with' works down the corridor and that she will have left her door open as she was grasping my oeuvre in her hand when she came to talk to Kirstie. I can make my escape via the window.

My paws scamper towards the closing door. I squeeze through the gap and then I run to the door of Angela's office. She's not there. I hear her haranguing someone on the other side of the wall. I leap on to a box, clamber up to the window, and escape to the outside.

However, I'm intrigued as to what might happen next. I decide to lurk and observe with my ears. Cats exhibit both these behaviours a lot and it's one way we learn about humankind and life. I also need to calm down a bit as I'd felt nervous in the main section of the library. I could have been trapped in there all night and my new owners might have thought I'd left for good and found a replacement who would eat all my food. A conversation in the office interrupts my thoughts:

"I never use your photocopier, I have a photocopier of my own, why would I use yours, when I have mine?" a small man wearing glasses is saying, presumably the Roger spoken about earlier.

"You have a cat at home, and I am willing to bet that this is your cat's arse," says Angela, pointing at my masterpiece of light and shadow, of fur and skin, of texture and baldness.

"My cat is black all over, her head's black, her body's black, her legs are black, her tail's black, and amazingly enough, given all the information I have provided you with, her backside is black too." Roger folds his arms and looks annoyed. "This is not Pixie Frou's bum."

Pixie Frou sounded a lot nicer than Gemma. I glance up

and see the sky looks grey as though it's displeased with my unkind thoughts about Gemma.

"Well, where did these come from?" asks Angela. "Who put these images here, if not you?"

"Angela, it was nothing to do with me. Perhaps it was some schoolboys in the library. They found a cat magazine and played a prank on you."

"These images are not from a magazine, there are no page numbers, we do not keep magazines of cat bums in the library, in fact there's no magazine called Cat Bum Weekly or Playcat, the equivalent of Penthouse or Playboy, but meant for people who like felines. It wouldn't sell very well and the only people who would buy it would be perverts. This is an image from an actual cat, either that or the photocopier has thrown a wobbler and printed off the results of its own nightmares."

"We don't have a cat in the library. Someone would spot the animal, and why would it head up here? There are photocopiers on the main floor and one on this floor for the public to use."

"The only other possibility is that there's a phantom cat in the library which we're only able to see when it takes a photocopy of itself." Angela looks rather earnest when she says this, and I can't help thinking that with her imagination she should write books for a living.

"Yes, well, I will leave you alone with that thought," says Roger. "I think we will not resolve this conundrum. Perhaps the repairman might have a better idea?" With that he saunters backwards out of the office and then makes a dash down the corridor to his own office and then it sounds like he locks his door.

Angela places the images on her desk and after examining them again, she puts them in her inbox, a two-storey construction made from blue plastic, on a filing cabinet by the door. She then sits at her desk and weeps into her hankie. I am sorry for her; it's my fault because I became overzealous in my desire to produce a masterpiece of cat anatomy to rival those that Rubens had done for humans. Actually, not just Rubens, but Velazquez too. Those are the only two painters I know because my old owner only had two books of paintings, limiting my learning. I decide to make a tactical withdrawal as the sky has seen Angela crying and does the same. I slither down the vine and trot around to my house, where I know a seething Gemma will have been practising Sneer Level 6 all day to prepare for my return from the outside world. I follow Sid's advice and scamper over the roof, before balancing on the still open window and sliding onto the kitchen countertop in an ungainly heap, though my paws are still at 10 to 2.

I need a snack, but I have left no food in my bowl as I'd been hungry in the morning. Archimedes hasn't opened the fridge in my absence, so I decide to sleep on the top of the bookcase, in a defensible position, until the two humans come home, and I can hang around them for a while until Gemma's anger subsides. I jump up to the highest shelf and wedge myself between the books and the top of the bookcase. The complete works of Charles Dickens and Jane Austen are comfortable beneath my fur, and I am glad they were so devoted to their craft in 19th Century England. Who knows, one day I might read Great Expectations or Pride and Prejudice. Or even both books because I have ambition to improve myself.

The next thing I am aware of is that I'm being chased around the library by a woman with blue hair who is trying to swat me with several pieces of paper with the image of my rear on them. I jump up to hit a silver disc to open a door and then I hide under a shelf and then I am running down some stairs and jumping up to open another door. Eventually, she corners me in her storeroom. I'm trapped. She approaches me and says:

"You're difficult to track down. Please O Great Artist, sign these original works of yours for me, so that people will know they're the originals and that these aren't copies of the originals." I am pleased to do so and then I purr…

…which is when I wake up because John is stroking me under my chin. He then says in his funny accent:

"Come on, Freddie, you should have some tea with your friend Gemma."

I miaow because that is the last thing on the surface of the Earth I want right now, so I cling on to Charles and Jane as best I can. My front claws are in Sense and Sensibility and my rear claws in Hard Times. I try to keep my tummy as close to Oliver Twist as I can. However, his superior strength wins out, and he scoops me up like a large baguette and carries me down to the basement, where sure enough Sneer Level 6 is waiting. I am plonked down by my bowl, and I eat because I am hungry, and because Archimedes hasn't been too helpful today in opening the fridge.

As I swallow nervously, John's footsteps disappear upstairs.

"I don't know what's worse," she starts, "you fraternising with crows, who you should eat, or you being carried around by that half-wit human."

I continue to eat my food and ignore her.

"Don't you have anything to say?" she demands.

I munch a mouthful of kibbles ostentatiously so that Gemma can see I can't reply because my mouth is full, and my mum always told me it was rude and common to speak with your mouth full.

"Why aren't you speaking? Answer me you stupid cat."

I chew some meat because I'm an obligate carnivore and need vitamins from meat, especially if I chew the meat thoroughly like I am doing at this precise moment.

Gemma attacks me at that point. She swats me on the nose and calls me a lackey of fascism. I swat her on the nose and scratch her, all the time remembering to look up the word 'lackey'.

"Gemma, stop this," I say. "I was being kind to those crows, they're our friends, and they told me some useful information."

"Kind?" she says. "I'll show you where kindness gets you," and she leaps onto my head and it hurts, and I let out my distress miaow.

"Mmmmmmmmmmmmmmmmmmiiiiiiiiiiiiiiiiiiiiiiiaaaaaaaaaaaaa aoooooooooowwwwwwwwwwwwww."

John runs down the stairs and pulls Gemma from me by her collar. He shakes her and says, "Bad cat, naughty cat." Gemma yowls at him.

John picks up a towel and throws it over her as he doesn't want to be scratched by her sharp, vindictive, evil, malicious, spiteful, harmful, murderous, nasty, scythe-like, dagger-like claws and takes her to a small room and puts her, still wrapped in the towel, on the floor in the cell. He pulls the towel from her and closes the door. "You will stay in there until you learn to behave," he says.

Gemma hisses worse than a pit full of snakes who are upset.

John comes over to me – "Are you alright, Fred?" he says. I tilt my head and raise my eyebrows to show that I will catfully try to continue despite my suffering, like my mum had taught me. He looks at my head to make sure there is no blood and pats me. Once he's gone, I continue to eat my food. I eat the rest of Gemma's food too as she won't be needing it, and use her litter tray, as she won't be needing that either.

I stand outside Gemma's temporary cell with my paws at 10 to 2.

"Gemma, I know you don't want to hear this, but kindness does work. The humans are nice, and the crows are friendly. I am going to make friends with Holly the Hamster and Rufus the Squirrel too, because I believe that's how life should be lived, not in some hate-filled red mist."

With that I pad up the stairs and go to sit with the humans who are both reading books. Mary's book is a recipe for something called Red Thai Curry. John is reading Brighton Rock by Graham Greene. I haven't slept on this book yet, so I look on the shelves and find about a dozen of Mr. Greene's books together. They aren't as wide as Charles's and Jane's books combined, so I will have to curl up on top of Graham's books to make a comfortable sleeping place. The problems cats have. I settle close to John's left ear on the back of the sofa and start to read about Pinkie and his exploits. John is a slow reader and I find myself drifting off into a very pleasant sleep.

Chapter 3

T o d a y

WELL, IT'S THE NEXT DAY again, which is still today. How confusing is that? I wake up to find myself still on the sofa, but the book has gone. I want to read what happened next, but the book isn't on the shelf where it should have been, if everything was done in a neat and orderly fashion. What is the world coming to? Surely Mr. Graham Greene's books should all be together for company? Why orphan a perfectly good book like that? Then I notice the living room door is closed. I can't go and have my breakfast and I can't use the litter tray. This isn't good, this isn't good.

My mum used to tell me to make the most of my time and not to mope if things didn't appear to be going my way. I remember those words as I sit trying to open the door of the lounge with my paw. There isn't enough room for me to insert anything under the door, so I resolve to make better use of my time. I hope to visit more of the library and find some interesting books on philosophy, religion, ancient history, and geography. However, what I should do first is inspect the bookshelves here in my new abode to see what I can read here, as long as I can remove the books from the shelf without knocking off any of the ornaments that are in the way.

I jump on to the back of the sofa and start my inspection. Charles's and Jane's books I already know about. And Graham's too. There are two long shelves of Agatha Christie, about 75 books in all. I see they are books featuring detectives called Poirot and Marple. I have never read a detective book before and it's a mystery why that is, but I resolve to start soon – perhaps I will start with *Cat Among the Pigeons* because there should be at least one character I can identify with.

On another shelf are twelve books by Eric Ambler who wrote thrillers according to the blurb on the back of one of his books. Most of them are set just before World War II when the world was even more dangerous than it is today. A few isolated titles by Daniel Defoe, George Eliot, Jonathan Swift, and three different types of Bronte complete the bookshelf.

These are all fictional books and there are 152 of them to read, which should keep me going for a while if I want to lose myself in a fictional world.

On the next bookshelf are the books about real things. Books about facts. Books about religions especially Eastern religions such as Hinduism, Shinto, and Zen Buddhism. Volumes on philosophy fill one row, mainly lists giving high-level explanations about the teachings of philosophers from Socrates to Bertrand Russell. A book of maps called an atlas intrigues me as all neighbouring countries are outlined in different colours, but this makes sense because how would you otherwise know whether you were in Germany or

Denmark other than by checking the colour of the ground under your feet, light blue for Germany and pink for Denmark? Another row of books are on ancient history from the Babylonians to the Egyptians to the Greeks to the Romans. Science completes the factual bookcase with books on neutrinos, anti-matter, and parallel universes. This is all wonderful news, and I can't wait to get started, but I do need to revisit the library to compare and contrast the books here with the books there. I should also make sure the blue-haired librarian is fine and has stopped crying.

A noise on the other side of the door attracts my attention and I immediately feign sleep on the floor with my paws tucked up to my tummy and chest. The door opens and the male human comes into the room:

"Oh look, he's still asleep. He's still convalescing from yesterday." John comes across and rubs my tummy, which I enjoy for about 5 seconds, before realising that the thing is empty. My tummy is empty and there's a gurgling sound to emphasise the point.

"Come on, Freddie," he says, "that nasty Gemma cat is still locked away, so you can enjoy your food in peace and poo to your heart's content."

This sounds like feline heaven, and I scamper downstairs with no second invitation. Gemma's bowl is empty but mine is full of important nourishment for my future growth as a distinguished cat. I've decided that as a Buddhist cat, who knows, maybe even a Zen Buddhist cat, I should not gulp my food but should eat serenely, calmly, slowly, and with respect. I approach the bowl and give it a little bow, before selecting each kibble individually and swallow it whole. The meat parts I decide to chew 42 times, because I once read a book that said 42 was the answer to everything. Eating in this respectful manner seems to take a lot longer, but by the time I've finished the humans have gone out to work and I feel full, because my brain has registered the fact my stomach is full of food. In fact, I leave some food in the bowl for later, which is unheard of for me. However, it makes sense because I can now have a sleep for 2 hours or so and then have a quick snack before getting some exercise, and using up those calories, by trying to climb the vertical rose staircase and then heading up the vine to the library window, a gentler incline with less chance of being affected by gravity. Talking of gravity, I should find a book on gravity in the library, so I can discover how to recognise it before it sneaks up on me and causes me to fall off things. Wherever it comes from, it's very quick to take advantage of my predicament and I end up landing on my paws with a surprised look on my face.

I decide to try and sleep on some more books in the hope I can absorb their teachings when asleep. I determine the Philosophy section would be one to try and I crawl in between the books and the shelf above. At the end of the row, one book is taller than the rest and so acts as a pillow. This is called *The Republic* by Plato and contains many of his other works too. I rest my head on this book and fall asleep immediately. I have strange dreams about old white men with beards asking and answering questions while waiting for someone to die by drinking something poisonous. Some sleep is restful, some sleep is relaxing, but this sleep is energy-sapping and when I wake up my head is spinning. Scanning the books, I decide to sleep in the other direction next time, as then my head would be resting on a selection of Sufi poems about love. I might be able to dream about my mum.

I head downstairs and eat my snack in my new respectful manner. I wonder if I should bow to each kibble before I eat it. I decide this is appropriate given what I appear to have absorbed from the philosophy books. It takes time to perfect the technique though I get the impression the kibbles are happier to be eaten this way, as though by nodding to them in turn I am recognising them as the individuals they are rather than crunching them to pieces in an anonymous way. Feeling sated, I run up the stairs and head for the window, which is open the same amount as it was the previous today. I jump down onto the grass and gaze up at the rose staircase. I can feel the food in my tummy telling me I can do this. I put my paws on the wire and pull myself up. I do the same action again and now all my paws are on the vertical staircase. I miaow to give myself some encouragement. Halfway up the staircase my strength gives out and I drop to the grass. I do a lot better than yesterday, and I will do better tomorrow.

"That was better," says the crow standing next to me.

"Thanks, Sid," I reply.

"I'm Stan," says Stan, "Stan the Crow, pleased to meet you."

"Pleased to meet you too, but how do I tell you apart?"

"Sid's got jet-black feathers, whereas mine are just very dark grey," says Stan.

"They look black to me," I reply.

~ 49 ~

"Well, they're not, Freddie, they're very dark grey and I think your eyes need to adjust to the subtle nuances of the darker items in the colour palette."

"I see," I say. "Can I just stare at your feathers a minute then?"

"Of course," says Stan, "time is not pressing on me greatly at this precise moment."

I stare at Stan's feathers and eventually see what he means, they are a charcoal colour of dark grey.

"How are things today, Stan?" I ask.

"Things are going well, today, young Freddie," replies Stan, "we had a good meeting with Rufus this morning about the nut and seed situation in the park and how it can benefit all of us in the long run. We exchanged information about where our caches of food are, so we don't steal each other's food. Apparently, there's a new squirrel in the park called Bertrand and he's been trying to find our caches, so we attacked him this morning and made sure he understood to create his own food cache rather than take someone else's."

"What's a cache?" I ask.

"It's a store of food that we keep hidden and we go and use that once the ground is hard and we can't get as much food as we'd like."

"That's a clever idea," I reply. "If you ever become short of food I can smuggle out some kibbles for you, if you'd like, it wouldn't be many, and I would have to carry them in my mouth and then spit them out of the window."

"That is very kind of you, Freddie, we might take you up on that idea later in the year."

"I know where they keep the kibbles in the kitchen, and I can stick my mouth into the bag and scoop out enough to keep you going for a few hours."

Stan nods his appreciation. "Speaking of kindness, where's the other cat that lives in your house, the vindictive, nasty, sneering one?"

"She's in solitary confinement for attacking me yesterday," I say. "She's in the slammer as I think they say, where she belongs."

"Were you hurt?" asks Stan.

"My feelings were hurt more than anything. I try to be kind to my fellow creatures all the time and I succeed most of the time, whereas Gemma tries to be unkind and horrid all the time and succeeds at being unkind and horrid all the time. It's practice I believe."

"She has chased us in the past, when she's been out in the garden, but I got the impression she doesn't like the wind blowing her fur and she doesn't like getting wet either. That means there are only a few days a year when she will venture outside."

"I think her kittens were taken away from her when she was younger, and she didn't get over the feeling of loss and separation. She should see a psychologist really and talk about her loss rather than taking it out on other creatures, who aren't to blame. I have to remember I'm not the target of her anger, I just happen to be around when she's feeling upset."

"Where are you off to today?" asks Stan. "Back to the library?"

"Yes, I want to find out how the blue-haired librarian is

feeling, she was crying yesterday, and I want to make sure she's OK. I also want to find out what books are in the library that I can read. The humans have a good selection and there's plenty of reading material for me, but those books need to be placed in a wider context of what books are available as a whole for me to read and that means going to the library and taking stock of the book situation. Unfortunately, I will probably have to be seen by some humans, but I hope they think I'm a ghost because the staff believe the library is haunted by a cat. I will have to keep moving and have exit plans for all eventualities."

"The front entrance doors slide open," says Stan, "and they're operated by pressure pads in the ground, so that when the humans place their feet on those pads, the doors slide open. No offence, Freddie, but you won't weigh enough to make those pressure pads work, so either you'll have to jump up and down a lot to make them work or jump from a height onto the pads. Now on the inside, there's two tall sensors which detect when someone is trying to steal a book from the library. What you could do is climb to the top of one of those sensors and take a leap onto the ground. That should operate the pressure pads."

"Thanks for the tip, Stan, it's very kind of you to mention that. It's the sort of thing Gemma wouldn't tell me. Anyway, I should be going."

"I will tell Sid to arrange a lookout for you at the front of the library. Either he or Seb will hang around at the front to make sure you're OK and to help if they can."

"How will I recognise Seb?"

"He's got beautiful dark-blue feathers, Freddie, just look at them for a minute and you'll see what I mean. He's really good at making a noise, creating a diversion, which will be useful if you're making a quick getaway."

"Thank you, Stan," I say, "I will see you soon."

Stan turns and makes a loud cawing sound. There are two replies from crows I can't see, presumably Sid and Seb. It is good to know I have friends in high places.

I scamper around to the back of the library and find the start of the vine path. I make measured progress up to the window. I jump on to the ledge and place my ear to the glass. There are two people talking, one of whom is Angela. I take a risk and look into the room. She is sitting at her desk whilst a man with a large bag of tools is examining the birthing mechanism of the photocopier.

"The thing is, Barry," Angela says, "I don't see how the machine could spontaneously emit a piece of paper with this image on it. Is that possible?"

Barry scratches his head with his right hand and then his bottom with his left hand before replying, "My professional opinion is that this photocopier could not do that without some outside assistance, namely a creature of some kind operating the machine by pressing the red button. However, the problem there is, looking at the log of commands, it would seem that the creature was able to operate the photocopier straightaway, without any false starts. In other words, whoever or whatever used this photocopier yesterday... knew how to operate it. And that is a bit scary from my point of view, because animals don't use photocopiers in nature…" he uses his left hand again…"and so how did the creature know what to do, which button to press?"

Barry forgets that animals have eyes and can observe these things taking place when humans operate the machine.

Angela continues, "Could a ghost have operated the machine, Barry, say the ghost of a cat?"

Barry ponders the philosophical question for several seconds without scratching any part of his anatomy before saying, "In my considered opinion, a ghost couldn't operate a machine like this because they're comprised of spiritual matter only, not physical matter, and wouldn't be able to apply pressure as such on the red button in order to operate the machine. That's just my opinion of course. If you're worried you should ask the vicar up the road, Reverend Clements, to come and perform an exorcism, to get rid of this spiritual visitor of yours."

"It's not just mine, it's a concern of the staff, or some of the staff on the second floor of the library."

This is useful information, the second floor of the library, so I have to go down two floors to escape out of the front entrance. Forewarned is forearmed as my mum used to tell me when I was a kitten. She was preparing me for just such a situation as this. My mum was really clever and able to see into the future.

"Well, I can't see anything wrong with the machine, so I shouldn't waste any more of your time and money," says Barry, starting to pack up his tools, "I think an exorcism is the best option and then you'll know there's no ghost operating the photocopier." With that he places some metallic objects into pockets in the bag and closes it.

"Well, thank you, Barry for your time," says Angela, "I should go home and walk the dogs."

"It might be a good idea to lock your office," says Barry, "and then no one could get in."

No, I think, *no don't do it, Angela, don't lock the office, please don't lock the office.*

"I can't today," says Angela, "Roger sent me an email to say he needs to come in and get some paper for his machine and as you know, for security reasons, only one person has the master key, the head librarian and she's on a course today."

"Well, at least close the door so that it looks locked," Barry suggests.

Barry is quickly becoming my worst thing in the world, as his suggestions might hinder my progress. If I had chance, I would place him in Room 101.

"Thanks, Barry," says Angela, "I'll do that."

I peek over the top of the window to see what is happening. Barry is leaving and Angela is putting on her coat. I observe closely how the door handle works when Angela closes the door. Once again, Archimedes isn't around when I need him most, so I, Freddie Cat, will have to work out how to get myself out of the predicament without an ancient Greek genius to help me unless he can work some magic with the gods.

I clamber over the top of the window, jump down onto a box, and then on to the floor. I pad over to the door and look at the handle. I hear footsteps in the corridor, this might be Roger as he's heard Angela leaving and doesn't want to meet her after their recent row, so I flatten myself against the wall just to the left of the door. Sure enough the door opens slowly, and Roger appears, looking a little hesitant. I thank Archimedes for his help and run into the corridor. I jump up to operate the silver plate on the wall and the door opens, taking what seems like an eternity to provide a gap large for me to skedaddle through.

There are more people around than the last time I was here, but luckily there is a shelf for me to hide under. I can see shelves of books to my left and the best way to get there undetected, or with the lowest risk of detection, is under the tables where the people are seated working away at their computers or reading books. In other words, they are distracted. I ready myself for the run under the desks. Three, two, one...and off I go, leaping over bags and avoiding swinging feet. I reach the shelves and take stock of my situation. Here is the Politics section with magazines and newspapers as well as books. There is a lot of politics and no humans, so I can observe the choice. I do a few test jumps onto the shelves and can only reach the lower two, the highest is out of reach. There are some gaps I can use to hide in when someone comes along to browse and occasionally there is a short cut for a cat to the other side of the shelf. Politics and Political History are duly noted in my mind. And now I want to go downstairs to the first floor.

A member of staff is coming my way pushing a trolley with two shelves, an upper and a lower. He is picking out books and placing them on the trolley. The lower shelf is almost full and the upper one clear.

Why would he be doing this? I wonder.

Then I remember that lazy people also use libraries and can't be bothered with the effort of finding a book themselves, so they ask the library staff to get the book for them, and then all the lazy person has to do is turn up at the front desk, present their library card, and the aforesaid book is pressed into their lazy hand with a 'Thank You'. This trolley is for the lazy people and my guess is that the man who is doing the lazy people's work for them would start at the top of the library and work his way down, so next stop first floor. When he comes to a halt again in the Politics section I creep onto the lower shelf and find a crevice between two books that I can hide in. Sure enough we proceed to the lift and the man presses the number 1. First floor here I come, in a trolley.

The doors close and there is a shudder as the lift heads downwards. At the first floor, the trolley heads towards the Geography and Travel sections, where I make my exit by Asia. As expected, Africa, North America, South America, Europe, and Australasia are close by. The first floor seems to be another fact floor. I find there are two sets of stairs and the ones at the back are very quiet because they are by the toilets. That's how I will descend to the ground floor. I sprint from Geography to History and consider the selection from a safe space in the Ancient Greece section. There are hundreds of books on Egypt, Italy, England, and Turkey.

Next to History is Science. I gaze at books on all the famous scientists including Einstein and Isaac Newton who it seems is responsible for gravity. He was hit on the head by gravity according to the book I see the blurb for and so it's his fault when I fall off fences and walls.

Why did you do that, Isaac, I wonder, *couldn't you have let gravity be?*

Next to Science is the Arts and books about all the artists other than Rubens and Velazquez I've never read about. There are books about renowned museums and famous statues. This leads to Architecture and then Archaeology. My head is beginning to burst with all the books on these subjects. I have to go downstairs and see what is there.

I scamper down the back stairs, holding my breath due to the smell, and arrive in the Children's section. No offence, children, but I'm not interested in your books at the moment. The ground floor is the fiction floor and not really of much interest to me. But I look anyway, as best I can as many people are on this floor. The problem is going to be exiting the establishment as there's a queue of people checking out their books.

Eventually, I find a gap on the shelves surrounded by other books. It is the perfect hiding place and allows me to lurk until the coast is clear. I am 10 yards from the escape doors. I see the sensors as Stan said and there is even a place I can jump from on to the pressure pads.

Then events start to go sideways. My perfect hiding place becomes no longer perfect. A lady takes out one of the books, making me visible to all and sundry. She looks at me and says, "Hello, Kitty, you must be the library cat," and then walks off to stand in one of the queues at the front desk. I watch her closely as I have a feeling she is the type of person who will mention meeting a cat in the library at close quarters. I ready myself for a rapid exit. When the woman starts talking to the librarian I observe very closely. Of course, the library cat is mentioned, and the librarian looks horrified. The woman points in my direction, and I have to leave. Timing is paramount. As soon as the librarian comes to my shelf, I have to leave. Pronto. The moment arrives.

"Where did you say you saw the cat?"

"Just here in the romantic fiction by Barbara Cartland."

The librarian starts pulling books out and I am exposed. I leave in a hurry. I jump on to the sensors and then down onto the floor. The doors stay closed. I do it again with the same result. Behind me someone says,

"Oh look, a cat seems to be trying to open the door by jumping on the pressure pads. How extraordinary."

I jump up and down on the ground and start to yowl, "Mmmmmmmmmmmmmmmiiiiiiiiiiiiiiiiiiiiiiaaaaaaaaaaaaaooooooo ooooooooooooooowwwwwwwwwwww." Then I notice that jumping on one particular floor tile causes the doors to shudder slightly as though they are thinking about opening. I decide to make their mind up for them. I catapult onto the sensors and then high into the air, before landing with all four paws and a few yowls on the floor tile. The doors open and I leave with the librarians close behind. However, they don't get far because Seb and Sid come to my rescue, chattering, squawking, and dive bombing the humans. I sprint round the side of the library and hide in the undergrowth. It would have been a mistake to lead my pursuers to my new home. The crows are still kicking up a fuss and so no humans come to find me.

After 5 minutes, I walk nonchalantly from my hiding place back to my garden. I wait for the crows to find me.

"How are you, young Freddie?" asks Sid. "They almost got you there."

"Yes, they did, but thanks to you and Seb they didn't," I reply.

"Congratulations on your escape," says Seb flapping down gently close by, "I managed a direct hit on one of the librarians for you as they were heading your way. One of the other humans said that you were an apparition, a material emanation of a spiritual being, so I hope you're proud of that."

"It sounds quite a compliment," I reply, "but I think I should avoid the library for at least 2 todays after today, to allow the humans to calm down. I will miss photocopying my rear end, but I have to be disciplined in these matters. In fact, on my next visit I will just photocopy my rear end and then leave again. That will give them something to think about."

"Perhaps you could photocopy another part of your anatomy to play with their minds a little more, to make them believe there's more than one material emanation?" suggests Seb.

"What a wonderful idea," I say, "thank you, Seb, I will do that, I will stand on the photocopier so they'll see just four paws one today and then the next today I will copy just my tail. That will confuse them no end and they might decide there's a whole family of material emanations living in their library. Living's not the right word, haunting sounds better."

"I like the word 'haunting'," says Sid, "it sounds shadowy and ethereal and otherworldly. Oh, here's the rest of the family come to say hello. There's Abigail..."

"Hello, Abigail, let me try and stare at your feathers so I can recognise you when I see you next..." I stare at Abigail's feathers and find them a combination of black and dark grey.

"And Henrietta..."

I stare at Henrietta's feathers...black and dark blue

"And Wendy..."

I stare at Wendy's feathers...dark grey and blue.

"And Stan you know."

"Hello, Stan."

"We should indulge in an identity parade for you, young Freddie," says Sid, "you turn your back, and one crow will be standing there when you turn around again, you have to identify which one."

"Yes, lovely idea." I turn around and count to ten. I turn back and stare.

"Abigail."

"Correct," says Sid.

I turn around 1.2.3.4.5.6.7.8.9.10.

I turn back.

"Still Abigail," I say, "you're trying to trick me."

Abigail caws with delight, "Well done, Freddie."

I play the game five more times and identify each crow successfully without any more corvine trickery.

"That was fun, young Freddie, we should be heading off

soon for a bit of exercise flying around the park before settling down for the night. We'll see you tomorrow."

"You will, Sid," I say, "and thank you so much for your help, all of you, you are contributing greatly to my education."

========

WHEN I SLITHER BACK INTO the kitchen, I am surprised.

"Hello, Freddie Cat, where've you been? I saw you with those crows," says Mary, "you seemed to be getting on well with them."

My heart skips a beat, as I had no idea my re-entrance to the property was being monitored by the humans.

I miaow and blush, but as my face is furry, it isn't visible to Mary. I look at the wall for a few seconds.

"I'll give you some food, now, Freddie, and then you should go upstairs before we let Gemma loose. She needs to eat and use the litter tray but don't worry, she will be back on her own for another night. She has to learn her lesson and be more tolerant of other animals."

I agree with her completely. Tolerance is not Gemma's strong suit. In fact, in her paw, she has no tolerance cards, no nice cards, and no happiness cards, it is all nastiness cards at the moment. Nastiness is her strong suit though it pains me to think this, as I know she's suffering inside. There must be some more cards in the deck to deal her.

"Speaking of litter trays, there's a smell in here," says Mary, "and I wonder where it's coming from?" She walks around the kitchen and stops by the cupboard with my first litter tray on top of it. She wrinkles her nose, and her hazel eyes look at me with curiosity, especially when she removes a peanut from one of the spikes. I blush again because I think she suspects me of doing something. She is right, but it wasn't really my fault. I didn't know and I improvised. I decide to look cute and hope she decides to feed me. She looks at me again and then walks to the fridge. I position myself for the best possible view of the interior. As she opens the door, I crane my neck and see there are no large fruit inside. That is a relief, no thuggery for at least 2 more days.

I follow Mary down the stairs with my tail pointing at the ceiling. I have often wondered why my tail follows me around all the time, I don't do anything so fascinating that warrants its interest, its devotion, but at least it's there when I need it. Although, the only use it has is to cover my front paws, which is a waste because I like to show my neatness via my front paws and their position. I have now trained my tail to hover above my front paws when I sit down, like a shelf or mantelpiece, emphasising the paws and drawing attention to their existence and their neatness.

Mary pours out the kibbles and scoops out plenty of food from the tin. She is generous with her portions whereas John is stingy. I prefer her feeding me. She has nice hands too and they caress me as I prepare to eat, remembering my new technique of respect for each individual kibble. I watch her go upstairs and then have a quick poo before commencing the food ceremony. I bow to the bowl and start to pick up each kibble and to swallow it whole. I am a lot hungrier than

I'd realised after the excitement of the library, but the discipline of my religion shines through and I complete my eating with some kibbles still left for later, whenever that may be. I lick my chops and decide to saunter upstairs to the lounge where I can decide which book to read on the next today.

In the lounge area, the bookshelves are placed strategically for the humans and not for felines. I would much prefer to sit on the back of a comfortable couch or chair and survey the books than sit on a hard, wooden floor facing the bookshelf as that would be described as 'unusual behaviour' by humans. It would be easier to sit on the back of the couch – a perfectly acceptable pastime for cats – and sneak glances at the books. In the end, I decide to sit on the arm of the chair and face the wall, so that I could look at the books in some comfort. I find the wooden floor causes cramps in my legs and doesn't aid my digestion, plus my tail sticks out at an angle and might be stepped on by a clumsy human foot. Facing the books means having my back to both the door into the outside world and the door into the kitchen. This is acceptable as Gemma is still imprisoned and I can see reflections of both doors in the windows giving me some forewarning should something hostile be heading my way such as a human wielding a jackfruit, though that will be in the future and not today, unless they're hiding the fruit.

As I begin to survey the books the door into the outside world opens and John enters. He has taken his shoes off in the porch and so is wearing just socks making his movements difficult to judge, a sneaky move to put me off my guard. I manage to extend my claws into the chair fabric just before he tries to lift me up. Luckily, he notices my attachment and contents himself with stroking me. I purr enthusiastically so that he will go away happy and leave me to my important deliberations regarding reading material for the future. My purring works and he heads off into the kitchen closing the door behind him.

Looking at the shelves, I have a decision to make. Which books can I reach from the floor, which from the arm of the chair, and which would I have to push out from above? The last option is my least favourite as it would involve some leaping on my part and some pushing of the book on to the floor below, which might upset the book and cause it some hurt. I have to respect the book and the words inside which the author will have worked hard to create. However, there are some obstacles in the way of the books on the lower two shelves, namely porcelain figures of cats, Oriental bowls, and small bottles of whisky which really belong in a drinks' cabinet. I would have to paw these to one side in order to obtain my chosen reading material. There are no ornaments on the top shelf and so it seems like a good idea to start reading books on this shelf first, even though it will involve leaping and noise. The next choice would be the lowest shelf of all, where I could practice pawing items to one side. This would involve delicate movements of one of my front paws, probably the left-hand paw, and gently shunt the ornament to one side. Practising on the shelf closest to the ground would be what's called a damage limitation exercise should I make a mistake and paw too much, resulting in the ornament leaving the bookshelf and landing on the floor where hopefully it would roll around and not break.

I stand up and start to look at the books on the top shelf. There was a choice between Charles Dickens, Jane Austen, and three books on Zen Buddhism. The three Buddhist books weren't there the previous today when I'd fallen asleep on top of Charles and Jane. This shows me that a greater power is at work and that my life as a Buddhist cat is the right path for me to take – the books are coming to me! Having said that, I think that I should read one of Charles's books and then one of Jane's followed by a book on Zen Buddhism. Reading a Buddhist book would allow me to confirm that I am living my life the correct way with respect to my fellow animals, my food, and the environment.

I leap on to the top of the bookshelf and look down on Charles's books. Which one should I choose? I extend a paw to test which of the books would come out the easiest. At this moment, the kitchen door opens, and John and Mary stand staring at me. John is holding Gemma who is wearing a mask over her mouth.

I think quickly, stand on my back paws, and start swatting the air, a bit like King Kong in the famous film of the 1930s.

"Oh look," says John, "Freddie is trying to swat a fly, make sure you catch it, Freddie."

"Freddie," says Mary, "look at Gemma, she will be spending one more night on her own and then she will be allowed out. She will be wearing a mask for another day and some claw coverings until she learns to behave properly."

I stop swatting the air and look at Gemma who appears

like a feline version of Hannibal Lecter – my knowledge of classic films is quite good for a cat – and I feel sorry for her, even though she is giving me a Sneer Level 6.

I miaow and the three of them disappear into the kitchen. I continue the search for a book and conclude that *Hard Times* is the best choice. It will land on the floor, and I can then start reading, although another problem has now presented itself. How to replace the book on the bookshelf? Could I carry it in my mouth and drop it on the bookshelf after reading some of it? I would try. Another option would be to paw it under the chair and then start reading the next today.

I am falling asleep and so make myself comfortable on the back of the couch. I would avoid the library for a few days and might even visit Holly the Hamster in the morning before reading in the afternoon. I would see how the mood took me. With that I put my chin on my front paws and am soon in dreamland.

Chapter 4

Today

I WOKE UP ON THE back of the couch with the sun streaming through the blinds and illuminating the varnished floor. The kitchen door is open, and I scurry through to the downstairs for a poo and to eat my remaining kibbles saved from the previous day – the benefits of disciplined eating, thanks to my religion! The humans come down to clean the litter trays and to put some food in our bowls. I chew the meat carefully and eat the kibbles individually. John brings Gemma and places her by her bowl. He takes off the mask and Gemma eats. She consumes more than one kibble at a time, which is disrespectful. She is now wearing some socks that cover her claws. The humans observe as we eat, no doubt concerned that Gemma might try to bite me. I doubt she will as she is a clever cat and knows that if she attacks me again, she will go back to the cat shelter or even worse be taken to the vet for an examination, most likely involving a thermometer being rammed up her rear end to take her temperature. Once again, I am full before I finish all my kibbles, even though John has shortchanged me as usual, and so I bow to the bowl and trot back upstairs.

I go to sit on the chair in the kitchen to make sure there are no jackfruit in the fridge. John comes over to me.

"Are you OK, Freddie, you didn't eat all your food?" he asks.

I miaow to assure him I am fine and to let him know that Buddhist cats have the discipline to leave food for later in the day rather than consuming all the food for the sake of eating it, which is greedy, wasteful, and materialistic. I also explain that not all cats are like Gemma and wolf their food down due to lack of self-control. This is true because I used to be like that too until I discovered myself.

He rubs my head, and I purr loudly to reassure him. As he walks over to the fridge, I jump down and stretch, allowing me a view of the interior. What I see upsets me a lot. There is a large fruit in the fridge, sitting proudly on the centre shelf. It is round and mainly green, with veins running from top to bottom. I don't believe jackfruit are completely round, they're more rounded in a rectangular way, but I should check in the dictionary at the library to be sure. Would the humans attack us with large fruit other than jackfruit, I wonder? I suppose there is a first time for everything.

I trot into the lounge and position myself on the couch where I remain as John and Mary leave for work. I jump onto the top of the bookcase and paw at *Hard Times* until it falls on the floor. I descend and apologise to *Hard Times* for giving it a hard time and a headache before bowing to it. I have a quick scan through the book and there are some English dialect words and local accents included. Either that or the printer wasn't good and missed certain letters from the beginning of some words irregularly. I also have a quick practice about biting the book and jumping onto the top of the bookshelf to gauge whether I can replace the book in a convincing manner. This proves to be difficult and *Hard Times* experiences two more trips to the floor – hard times for *Hard Times*. I abandon the idea of replacing the book as it is getting soggy from my mouth, so I leave it in the sunshine to dry out.

Through the kitchen window I see Holly the Hamster in her cage in the house next door. As I'm a disciplined eater, I maintain my svelte figure and as a result I'm able to exit via the kitchen window. I jump down to the grass and try to haul myself up the staircase. This time I almost make it to the top before falling off in an elegant and controlled manner. The crows are over in the park by the sound of it, probably sorting out the squirrel who is eating their cached food. I trot across the grass to the fence, jump up and spring on to the window ledge where I can view Holly. She stops running in her wheel and turns towards me.

"Hello, Freddie, how are you?"

"I'm well," I say, "how do you know my name?" I blush under my fur and stare at the wall for 10 seconds.

"Sid told me. I've heard about your exploits at the library with the humans and the photocopier. Could you take me to the library one day, I've never been inside a library?"

"Of course, Holly. You can ride on my back as I climb up the vine on the outside wall. But how would you get out of there, out of your cage?" I return my gaze.

"Sometimes my humans, Matthew, and Monica, forget to close my cage properly and I can escape if I want to, but I'm addicted to exercise and so I don't want to. However, a trip to the library sounds appealing, so if I give you a signal then can we go over?"

"Of course, Holly. What form will the signal take?"

"Well, young Freddie, I normally run towards the south as I was this morning, but if I am running to the north, then you should understand my cage is unlocked and I can go for an adventure with you."

"So, if you're running towards the park then it's adventure time?" I say.

"That's correct, Freddie, but you won't be bringing that horrible cat that lives with you on the adventure, will you? She'd want to eat me."

"I promise I won't bring Gemma; besides, adventures are beneath her, Holly, and she's too fat to get out of the window. She hasn't the discipline to keep her body slim."

"Oh, that's good to hear, Freddie. Everyone is very wary of her. Gemma, did you say? She's nasty, even the plants don't like her."

"How do you know that?" I ask as I wasn't aware that plants had feelings about cats.

"The trees communicate with each other, and the plants do too. Gemma pees on the plants when she goes outside rather than on the soil and the plants don't like it. As you say, she only goes out when her humans let her, which isn't often, but she creates a terrible impression when she does."

"That is Gemma. She doesn't care about anything else. Anyway, on a nicer subject, do you like art, Holly?"

"I do, Freddie, why do you ask?"

"I thought we might create some art on the photocopier, because I reckon the librarian likes the items I've produced because she's told so many people about them."

"What do you do, Freddie, that so impresses them?"

"Well, Holly, I sit on the top of the photocopier with my tail sticking out so that it copies my rear end when I press the red button. I have to make sure the 'Print on both sides' option is set."

Holly giggles so much that she stumbles off her wheel and lands in the straw.

"That's funny, Freddie," she says crawling back on the wheel, "I bet that worried them, when they saw that."

"I'm not sure it was worry, more surprise," I say. "Anyway, I was wondering whether we could both sit on the photocopier at the same time. I'll press the red button and let's see what we produce. It will be a work of art, a post-modern statement, a surrealist masterpiece."

"We'll need a giraffe if you want it to be surreal," says Holly, "and I haven't seen too many of those around here."

"Neither have I," I reply, "but then again I haven't been looking for a giraffe. Maybe you have to look for a giraffe to find one."

"Well, that is true, Freddie, you have to search for things sometimes."

"What do your humans do?" I ask.

"Matthew is a dentist and specialises in root canal surgery and Monica is an accountant for a bank. They don't have any children as yet, but they'd like to have two or three at some point. What about your humans, Freddie?"

"She writes technical words, and he analyses businesses."

"He's a psychoanalyst for businesses? He must need a large couch for that."

I miaow with laughter.

"They're quite nice," I continue, "and they've been kind. Gemma attacked me for being stupid, ignorant, sycophantic, and collaborative, so they put her in a room on her own for 2 days to calm down. They were protective of me, which is lovely. My mum would have been happy for me."

"What happened to your mum, Freddie?"

"They took me away from her when I was young, and I was given to an old lady. I never saw my mum again. It makes me cry sometimes when I remember her. I hope she's alright and I hope she still remembers me."

"I'm sure she does, Freddie, she'll think about you every day and she will hope that you're happy."

"Do you think so?"

"I do, Freddie, she'd be so proud of you, the way you've turned out. She brought you up well, didn't she?"

"I hope so. I was very lucky to have such a good mum. Do you remember your parents, Holly?"

"I don't, Freddie, all I can remember was living in a shop and then being sold to Matthew and Monica about 15 months ago."

"Are you happy here?" I ask, looking around at the view from the window ledge.

"Yes, I am happy, but I am pleased you've arrived, as it's great to have another perspective. The crows are funny and keep me amused. Rufus lets me know what's happening in the park on the other side of the road, somewhere I'll probably never see."

"I've never been to the park, Holly. Once I've been perhaps we could go together along with Rufus, because Rufus knows how to cross the road and not get squashed, which is very important."

"That would be wonderful, Freddie, but I'd like to go to the library first, just to be in a place with so much knowledge all around would be an amazing experience for me. I've always wanted to visit Egypt."

"We've got it all arranged, Holly, and talking of the library I should go there now, as I have to look up some information about fruit. Do you know anything about jackfruit?"

"No, Freddie, I know little about fruit, and I don't eat fruit other than the occasional slice of apple. What is it you want to know?"

"Well, Gemma says the humans are fascist jackbooted thugs, but I looked in the dictionary at the library and I couldn't find jackboot, but I found jackfruit, so I must have misheard her. Anyway, I looked in the fridge just before I came over here and I saw a large fruit, a striped round one, and I wondered if that was a jackfruit, because if it is then the trouble could start soon."

"I think Gemma is biased and over-reacting. You say yourself the humans were kind to you, so why would they throw fruit at you? They might throw fruit at Gemma, and you could understand that, but not at you, Freddie, you're too kind."

"Thank you, you're right, Holly, but I'll go over anyway, as I want to make more art. Bye, Holly."

"I will see you later, Freddie," says Holly and runs on her wheel.

Having said our goodbyes, I jump onto the fence, leap down onto the grass, and then scamper around the edge of my garden towards the library. I run through the garden gate and scurry along the footpath, keeping a low profile. Having spoken to Holly, I decide to treat the vine with respect. I bow to it and ask whether I might use it as a staircase to the library window. There is a slight breeze, and the plant shifts its position. I retract my claws and climb up the main stem, using the smaller stems as steppingstones. I reach the top and stop to listen and lurk.

Angela is eating a sandwich and reading a magazine about archaeology. I find a comfortable position and wait for her to walk her dogs. I notice that the photocopier lid is vertical, showing my artist's palette is available for use. After munching her sandwich with great respect, Angela leaves the room and locks the door behind her. I watch for a further 5 minutes and then enter the room by stealth.

I pad over to the dictionary and turn over the pages. The page that becomes open contains the word 'giraffe'. What a wonderful coincidence. I find jackfruit and then find a picture of a jackfruit, which I'd missed before in my excitement. To my relief, it looks nothing like the large item in the fridge. I am safe for now, although Holly is correct I'm sure about the humans' fruit-wielding intentions towards me. I am happier and jump onto the photocopier and create a masterpiece at the push of a button. The photocopier births my piece and then I scamper away to the window. I bow to the vine and thank it for being such a wonderful, natural staircase before nimbly descending to the ground. Before re-entering the house for an afternoon's reading of *Hard Times*, I decide to go to the gym by clambering up the wire underneath the window. I wonder if it would help my cause by bowing to the wire too as they made it out of metal and therefore it has a natural spirit even though a machine manufactured it with help from humankind. I decide it is worth a try. After all, it costs nothing for me to dispense my kindness and respect to whoever or whatever I choose. I bow to the wire mesh and then climb. It might be my imagination, but the metal seems softer and more giving under my paws, enabling me to climb more effectively and with less effort. I reach the top of the wire without too much difficulty and then clamber onto the window ledge. I feel pleased with myself, but then I remember what my mum had told me once – never gloat on your achievements, because you can always do better. I look down at the wire and wonder whether I could ever climb down it to the ground. I would have to go backwards and cling on to the window ledge with my front paws while finding a foothold with my back ones. That would take some practice, but I resolve to try.

I turn around and find Gemma is on the window ledge, looking at me. I clamber inside. Gemma gives me a Sneer Level 3, but says nothing, which is unusual for her. She thinks I am being ignorant and stupid, but that is her problem, not mine. She is no longer wearing the mask, but she is wearing the socks that stop her from clawing things such as myself.

I am hungry and go downstairs to finish my breakfast of kibbles. I bow to the bowl and chew each individual kibble.

"You are so pretentious, bowing to the bowl like that, anyone would think you were a Buddhist cat."

"I think I am," I say between kibbles, "I feel at peace and live in the moment."

"You need some mental strength. You should try to eat those crows and that hamster, not be friendly with them. Wherever did you learn that?"

"Where did I learn to be kind and respectful? Well I suppose from my mum, but also from my soul, because my soul has lived before and so fills me with its previous experiences in the universe."

"What utter rubbish," says Gemma, flicking her tail angrily, "you don't have a soul, Freddie. What you should try to do is tune in to the collective cat consciousness and learn from all the cats who've ever lived about their lives."

"How do you tune into that station?" I ask.

"It's not on the radio, you notice it and it fills you with love and pride for the way of the cat. You meditate to understand what you're being told from down the centuries."

"Is that what's happening when you appear to be staring out of the window for long periods of time?"

"You're being sarcastic now," says Gemma and gives me a Sneer Level 2.

"I respect what you're saying, but that doesn't work for me. How do you know where your thoughts are coming from? How do you know you aren't just in touch with your own soul that has lived before?"

"Because of all the different voices that fill my head, Freddie."

"But each voice could be from a different life. If your soul is immortal, it will have lived many times and so each voice is from a different life."

"You don't know that. That's just a guess."

"It's what I feel, Gemma, and I applaud you for having that belief, which makes you a well-rounded feline. It was nice talking with you, but now I want to read a book for the afternoon."

"Which book are you going to read?"

"It's *Hard Times* by Charles Dickens," I reply, "I've never read one of his books."

"How will you get the book back on the shelf?" asks Gemma.

"I'm going to keep it under the chair, because I haven't found a way of carrying it back up to the top shelf and placing it back where I found it."

"The humans will find the book and put it back because they don't want us to become educated and want to keep us down."

"I am not sure why they'd want to do that," I reply, "a book about Victorian Britain and the terrible treatment of the working class by the newly wealthy ruling elite will not make me want to overthrow the existing world order of the here and now. Even though it probably should because that's not a fair system."

"Let me know if that's what the book is about, I might be interested in that after all."

"I will, and it was nice talking with you, Gemma," I say and trot off to find *Hard Times.*

==========

AFTER READING *HARD TIMES* FOR 2 hours, I decide to take a nap. It is a fascinating book although I can't understand what the character called Stephen Blackpool is saying. I reckon the printer must have misprinted all his conversations or had run out of the letter 'H' as he drops most of his Hs in conversation. Perhaps there's censorship involved, or all the missing letters form a message of spiritual significance? Mr. Dickens might be cleverer than I realise. I will have to go back and check although whatever the secret message is, it will contain a lot of Hs – perhaps the secret message has a stutter? In which case we should sympathise with its suffering. And the character named Josiah Bounderby must surely be the basis for the Four Yorkshiremen sketch made by the Monty Python people, even though *Hard Times* is based on a town or towns in the county of Lancashire, which is nearly the same as Yorkshire but not quite. Its rose is a different colour. I saw that in a book. One was red and one was white, but I can't remember for sure which is which. I seem to remember Yorkshire is the White Rose county and Lancashire is the Red Rose county in which case the rose that goes to the gym outside the house is from Lancashire. I shall have to ask the rose about its origins the next time I see one of its flowers.

I am slumbering on the back of the couch when John

comes back from work. He sometimes acts as though I can reply to his statements and questions with sounds and actions other than a miaow. I will have to try mews, purrs, yawns, sniffs, and stretches to see whether this gets my message across. Anyway, on this occasion he comes across and strokes me under the chin before asking me, "You'll never guess what I've just seen, Freddie."

Of course I don't know what he's seen, because I was on the back of the couch with my eyes closed. I raise my eyebrows and sniff the air.

"There was a clergyman going into the library, but he wasn't looking for a book, he was going to perform an exorcism, because the library staff reckon the ghost of a cat haunts the library, a cat just like you, Fred."

Just like me. I hope not because my mum never mentioned I had a twin. A twin who had become a ghost. It sounds like an interesting job, haunting somewhere like a library.

At that moment Mary comes through the kitchen door, having sneaked in when I was asleep.

"Are you talking to the cat, you understand he won't reply?" she asks.

I stare at her with a knowing look and then miaow.

John smiles: "I was just telling Freddie the library is trying to exorcise the ghost of a cat that is haunting the library. A clergyman is there right now performing the exorcism. According to a member of the library staff, the ghost has been leaving signs on a photocopier on the top floor."

"Signs? What signs?" asks Mary. She reckons John is making the whole thing up.

"Apparently, and I am not making this up, the cat or the ghost cat I should say, leaves a representation of its arse on the photocopier, complete with fur and the underside of its tail." He cannot complete the sentence without giggling, a very juvenile reaction for a mature adult. It's not an acceptable way to refer to my masterworks of Impressionist painting. By Impressionist I mean the impression that my rear end has left on the glass.

"It photocopies its bum?" asks Mary.

"Yes." He can't stop laughing. I am a maestro of the photocopier as an art form, and I resent his lighter than light attitude towards my creativity.

"How? Ghosts are spirits, they have no mass, no weight to press down on the button to make the photocopier work. That makes little sense."

"Well, maybe the ghost cat has ways of making a book or something with mass land on the button, so that the photocopier works. Anyway, I think it's hilarious, especially when the library staff member says they chased the cat out of the library after they found it lurking in the Romance novels section." Again, he giggles. I yawn. This is accurate reporting and soon even the humans will put two and two together and make four. The four will be that my four paws have been in the library.

"Why would a ghost cat be in the Romance novels section, surely it would be in the Horror section or the Thriller section or the Ghost Story section?"

"Yes, it was obviously lost, poor soul, perhaps it's an emanation from one book in the library, a book that has a cat in it which passes away under unusual circumstances, perhaps the cat was run over by a photocopier, and this is the revenge it's exacting on the library housing the book."

"Your imagination is working overtime, John, and I feel that the library is being haunted by an actual cat." Mary looks at me pointedly and then goes back into the kitchen. I'm not sure what to make of her staring at me like that. She couldn't possibly work that out, as she was writing technical words when I was in the library. I am at peace about the situation as a Buddhist cat should be. John heads into the kitchen too, presumably to change out of his analysing business clothes.

I take the chance to look at some of the other books on the bottom shelves. One is *To the Lighthouse* by Virginia Woolf and another *Mrs. Dalloway* by the same author. There is *From the Earth to the Moon* and *20,000 Leagues under the Sea* by Jules Verne. These books have interesting pictures on the front, and I think I should read them. I apologise to Jane, but I will leave her books until later. Plus, books on the bottom shelf are slightly easier to replace on the shelves. There are 3 books on Eastern Philosophy, and I think I ought to read those to catch up on Taoism, Confucius, Hinduism, and Shinto. My old owner just had books on Buddhism, which I had read voraciously, but she obviously hadn't read them, because nowhere in those books does it say you should throw pets at vets in situations where you can't pay the vet to treat your pet.

I look across at Holly who is still running southwards and reflect that it has been a good day. Even Gemma had been passably nice, a miracle in itself. Tomorrow, I would go over to the park in the morning, assuming Rufus turned up on time, and I would discover what there was to see over the road. I wouldn't visit the library because I think I should give them a day's respite between hauntings. I would like to see what an exorcism involves, presumably holy words, holy water, a cross being waved about, and an exhortation for the ghost to vacate the premises. What I was doing was interpreted as the devil's work and so I had to use that power with care, otherwise the library might be closed, and I wouldn't want that, because Mary had mentioned some sections I hadn't seen – Horror and Ghost Stories – so I ought to find those on a future visit.

John pokes his head around the door from the kitchen.

"Your food is ready, Freddie cat."

I need no second invitation and scurry downstairs, probably too quickly because now they'll work out I understand what they're saying to me.

John has short-changed me with the food as usual, but he is hanging around to make sure that Gemma behaves herself. I have a poo and then begin the food ceremony by bowing to my plate. Gemma gives me a Sneer Level 3. I carry on regardless, chewing my wet food 42 times and then eating a kibble at a time.

"Are your teeth hurting you, Freddie cat? You're only eating one kibble at a time."

I am not sure that I can find the words to explain that as a Buddhist cat I am being respectful towards my food. In the interests of not going to the dentist, I eat three kibbles at a time, but swallow them one at a time. John moves to clean my litter tray and I can go back to individual kibble eating. After she has finished gobbling her food, Gemma gives me a Sneer Level 5 – Quisling cat – before going to sleep next to her designated bed. This is a protest on her part about the conditions she is living under.

I don't finish my kibbles again, because my stomach has registered with my brain that it is full. I should write a book extolling the virtues of Buddhism for maintaining a healthy weight in felines. That will be my next publishing project after this one, though I will have to come up with more meaningful headings than 'Today' for each separate section. That will tax me. Benjamin Franklin was correct about taxes. I go upstairs to think about how to approach this and fall asleep on the back of the chair without coming up with any definitive answers.

Chapter 5

Today

I HAVE SOME STRANGE DREAMS about walking in the library and all the characters from all the books coming out as ghostly apparitions to wave at me as I stroll past. Some of them dive bomb me before returning to the pages where they belong. I know whose fault this is, and I resolve not to listen to him in the future, but on this occasion my subconscious has played a trick on me during my long night's sleep. Walking in the Travel section, The Pyramids at Giza harassed me, as well as the Eiffel Tower, St Paul's Cathedral, The Coliseum in Rome, the Sahara Desert, the Taj Mahal, and the Great Wall of China. This was disconcerting and didn't give me a restful sleep. I wake up with a start. Mary is stroking my rear paws, and it is really nice. I purr and roll over twice, forgetting where I am. I land on the floor, earning a Sneer Level 2 from Gemma, who is sitting in the kitchen doorway.

"Come on, Freddie, let's give you some breakfast."

This is good news because it means a generous portion, so I trot after Mary, earning a change in Sneer Level from 2 to 4 from Gemma, who follows at a suitably distant distance that wouldn't earn herself a Sneer Level 4 if she looked in the mirror. Once again, a poo is the order of the day before eating. As I eat each kibble, I wonder if I should mention that order of events in the book or whether I should have a poo after I eat to understand whether I eat more, less, or the same. This is an important analytical equation. Would I eat as much if my body was full of food and ex-food that was still in me? The humans don't have any anatomy books, so another visit to the library is in order, though not today as I am hoping to meet Rufus at 9:55am to accompany him over the road. I hope to complete *Hard Times* before starting *To the Lighthouse*. I also have to go to the gym before seeing Rufus. And talk to the crows.

Once John and Mary have gone to work, I skedaddle out of the window and jump down onto the lawn. Sid is there to talk to me.

"Young Freddie, how are you?"

"I'm fine, Sid, how are you, where were you yesterday?"

"We were over in the park having a reckoning with the squirrel over there, the one I was telling you about."

"The one who was stealing your cache of food? The one called Bertrand?"

"That's the one. Well, we've banned him from the park. Our cousins over there Rob, Ron, Reg, Sue, Belle, and Jacqueline are making sure he doesn't come back. We pecked him a lot yesterday, and he was almost picked up by his tail. He left in a hurry."

"He sounds like a bad squirrel to me," I say, "with no consideration, respect or manners for other creatures. I'm hoping the good squirrel Rufus will take me over the road and into the park this morning."

"Well, we'll help you, we'll caw when the coast is clear, but really you should check both ways as you're walking across the road."

"Thank you for the advice, Sid. Did you know the library had an exorcism yesterday, to get rid of the ghost cat?"

"Yeah, we did. We actually watched through the window, me, and Stan. A man with a white collar uttered some holy words and bade the spirit leave the building forever. He set up a cross on the floor too. It was quite moving, though we had to giggle at the library staff because they were looking petrified. Neither me nor Stan felt the spirit leave the library."

"I understand. Well, I won't be visiting today so the library will reckon the exorcism has worked at least until tomorrow."

"Well, don't forget that Angela at the library works Monday to Friday, so that window won't be open tomorrow as it's Saturday tomorrow and your humans won't be going to work either."

"I didn't know that. I thought they worked every day."

"No, there was a strong trade union system back in England in the 19th and 20th centuries, which represented workers well, so they only worked 5 days a week. The employers gave them lunch breaks and holidays."

"They were organised, weren't they?" I reply.

"They were and you have to be to get things in life and stand up for yourselves. Being organised is the basis of crow society, stand together, fly together, hop together, and take care of each other."

"I try to be organised, but then again there's only me," I say.

"It's not necessarily easy to organise yourself. Be prepared to do things, motivate yourself, and not be lazy, young Freddie, give yourself credit."

"Thank you, Sid. I also try to treat everything with respect, including the metals on this staircase. I climbed up it yesterday when I treated it with respect."

"Go on, Freddie, show me."

"OK, I will, but please make sure that you vacate the landing area. I wouldn't want to land on you."

I bow to the metal obtained from Mother Earth and thank it for allowing me to climb up to the top. I put my paws on the wire and pull. It seems straightforward, as though the metal is lifting me upwards to the top. I reach the top and jump back down again.

"Have you considered climbing down as well?" asks Sid.

"I am not sure of where to start, really," I say. "I'm worried about getting my paw caught in the wire and hurting my leg."

"Well, we could help you there, Freddie, togetherness you see. We tell you where to place your paw so that you won't hurt yourself. We could do that on Monday. Anyway, Rufus will leave in about 5 minutes from his tree, so you should scamper, young Freddie, we'll help you over the road."

"Right, Rufus, yes I don't want to miss him crossing the road as I need his expertise. Does he charge animals for his guidance services?"

"No, Freddie, if you find a nut, give him that as a token of appreciation, but he's going over anyway, so you make sure you scamper along beside him and don't stop in the road."

"I will, thank you for the advice."

"We'll help, we'll squawk if there are no cars coming along."

"Thank you, Sid. Right, I will run over to Rufus's tree and wait for him."

"He's expecting you and I told him not to worry if there is a cat at the bottom of his tree at 9:55am."

"Thank you, Sid."

I head to the tree and wait patiently for Rufus to arrive. My paws are at ten-to-two, as my mum always taught me – no manspreading from me. At 9:55am, Rufus runs down the tree and comes over to me.

"You must be the Freddie cat everyone is talking about. I am so pleased to meet you. I'm Rufus. We should head over to the park. Now, it's important to follow me and my methods. When we cross the road, look left first and then right, in that order and make sure it's clear in both directions before crossing. Do you understand, Freddie cat?"

"I do, left then right, both directions clear, scamper across."

"Yes, you've got it. Do you have questions?"

"No, not yet."

"Right, let's head to the park, but first the road. We have to find a position where we can see both ways… there's a good place."

The crows are perched on some parked cars and

monitoring the traffic. Suddenly there's squawking. Rufus looks left and right, I look left and right, it's all clear, so we run across the road to the other side. The other side looks very similar to the side of the road where I live, with grass, flowers, and trees.

"Come on," says Rufus, "time to explore the park. We follow this path over the mound, and you'll see it."

We climb to the top of the mound, and I view the park for the first time. What a wonderful surprise. The park is oblong with a path all the way around with trees and bushes and some strange-shaped things I've never seen before.

"What are those odd things over there, the big yellow thing and those swinging things and the red round thing?"

"They are what's called a children's playground. The big yellow thing is a slide. You climb up the steps on one side and slide down the metal chute before falling off the end. The swinging things are swings because they swing if someone pushes you and you swing until you don't swing any longer. The red round thing is a roundabout and goes round and round when someone pushes you. With both swings and roundabouts, you need someone human-sized to push you."

"But not for the slide," I say, "because it sounds like gravity will push you for that."

"We'll finish at the playground. I will show you around first. The crows in the park know about you. Ron and Reg are Stan's cousins. There's no resident squirrel since yesterday because they banished him for stealing and he won't come back. They pecked him a lot. There are plenty of small birds who live in the bushes. Please don't catch them as they're all lovely, every single one of them."

"I don't catch birds," I reply, "it's against my religion, but I will try to say hello, especially to those that flap a lot."

"The hummingbirds?"

"Yes, they make a *zzzzzzzz* sound when they fly, and I like that noise."

"Well, don't scare them, they're highly strung."

"OK, I will treat them with respect and kindness like I do with all other creatures including Gemma."

"Be careful, because there are wasp nests in some trees, and they are evil creatures."

"The yellow and black insects that sting things? Yes. I've read about them, they are mean, but consistently mean, they don't show anyone any favours."

"And finally, this is a favourite place for people to walk their dogs, but we are usually OK at this time in the morning because most people walk their dog either before or after their work and not during the day."

"Yes, dogs are not my favourites, but I tolerate them. I reckon it must be terrible to be a dog and find every stick attractive, chase every moving thing, catch every round ball, bark at the slightest provocation, and be so weak mentally that I couldn't take a walk by myself because my owners wouldn't trust me to come back on my own."

"I know what you mean about dogs, Freddie, those are wise words indeed. Myself, I scamper up a tree if I so much as see one coming in my direction."

"Oh, Rufus, I'm sorry to hear that, what I do is arch my

back, get my hair to stand on end, and hiss with a yyyyyyyyyyyyyyyoooooooooooooooooooowwwwwwwwwww wwwwwwwwwwwwwllllllllllllllll sound. We could try practising that together if you like?"

"Right," says Rufus, "I will try." He arches his back and strains to make his fur move.

"That's not bad," I say, "but stick your tail in the air too, so it points upwards."

"How about I point the tail at the dog threateningly?" says Rufus.

"If you can do that," I reply.

Rufus shows me he can do it and I immediately try to copy, but without as much success as Rufus.

"Hissss," says Rufus.

"Breathe in more before you begin," I say.

"HHHHHHHHHHhhhhhiiiiiiiiiiiiiiiiiiiiiiiiiiiiisssssssssssssss."

"That's better, you should try practising in your tree, Rufus, like everything the more you practice, the better you will be at it. Oh, here are some crows, but these are the park crows, aren't they?"

"Yes, it looks like Ron, Reg, and Rob, a welcome committee for you, Freddie."

Three crows hop across towards Rufus and me. They stop about a yard away.

"Are you Freddie?" asks one.

"I am Freddie. I am pleased to meet you. Whom do I have the pleasure of addressing?"

"He is charming, just like Stan said," says the crow. "I'm Reg, this is Ron, and that's Rob."

"Morning, Freddie," say Ron and Rob.

"Pleased to meet you," I say. "I will just look deep into the colour palette of your feathers, so I can remember each of you individually, as I think that helps creatures get along." I stare at each crow for about 30 seconds. They stand still whilst I do this.

After I finish, I close my eyes and commit the palettes to my memory.

"Well, that's done," I say. "What's happening in the park today? It looks quiet."

"It is," says Reg, "but it will be busy later, Freddie, with people walking their dogs and other people lying around on the grass trying to roast themselves to a deep-brown colour."

"Humans are funny," I say, "why give yourself skin cancer just to look brown, they might as well coat themselves in mud."

"Or dog mud," says Rob.

"But they'd smell then," says Ron.

"They wouldn't get cancer," says Rob.

"True, Rob, true," says Reg, "wise words indeed – Rob is our philosopher and thinks deep thoughts, usually about dog mud, leaves, and nuts."

"And not always in that order," says Rob.

I giggle. This is fun and educational; travel broadens the mind.

"As you're over here, Freddie, we thought we'd give you a tour around the park and show you the highlights," says Reg.

"That is just what I want," I reply. "Lead on Reg, Ron, and Rob."

"Well, hop this way," says Reg, "and see what there is just over here."

We move towards three benches that give a view over a rugby pitch. These benches are under some small, scrubby trees. Humans have left some of their possessions behind, though there is a special name for these items – litter.

"You know your male human always does two things when he comes over here, which we are grateful for."

"You mean John comes over here? Does Rufus help him across the road?"

"Rufus doesn't help him. John's a human and can look out for the cars himself. He walks around the park and then runs away from this park to another park 3 or 4 miles away and then comes back."

"It's called exercise, isn't it?" I say. "It seems a waste of time to run all the way away, just to come back here again, he could have stayed here all the time."

"It keeps him fit, Freddie," says Rob. "It keeps the blood flowing to his muscles and keeps them healthy and strengthens his bones. It's like you climbing your staircase over at your house. That exercise keeps you fit and healthy."

"You've heard about that?" I ask. "I didn't think anyone else would be interested. Anyway, Reg, you say he comes over here and does two things you're grateful for? What are those, please?"

"He brings nuts and small seeds, especially in the winter, and scatters them where we can find them. He puts the smallest seeds in nooks and crannies, so only small birds can get them, which is fair enough because we've a thriving bird population in the park and this park is big enough to support them all. But he does that 5 mornings a week, and he picks up the litter, the plastics, the cans, the drinks containers, and puts them in the big bin over there. And that's good because it means those items don't pollute the environment and means we don't get our beaks stuck in them when we investigate them for food."

"He never mentions that," I say, "I suppose he's being modest."

"It's deeds that count not words," says Rob, "by your actions shall you be known."

"Yes, that makes sense, Rob," I say. "I will have to remember that – it is only our deeds that reveal who we are, as I believe Carl Gustav Jung once wrote. My first human owner, an old lady, once had a book of his on her bookshelf and I read it often."

"You're a very well-read young cat," says Rufus, "and you are lucky to have had some books to read. There's no room for any books in my tree."

"You should come to the library with me, Rufus," I say, "there are plenty of books there."

"I've heard that. I went up to that window where you gain entry, but I didn't have the courage to go in."

"Freddie here has plenty of courage," says Reg. "Shall we continue around the park?"

"There's a dog at 10 o'clock," says Ron, "although it's attached to a human, let's just be aware of it."

"It's a little runt of a dog," says Rob, "and might therefore try to make a name for itself and to enhance its feelings about its own lack of stature. I see the ladies have their eyes on it and are monitoring it closely."

"This might be an opportunity to enhance your hissing, Rufus," I say, "a little dog like that is a good place to start."

We animals walk along the grass towards a clump of trees where Reg stops.

"This is where we sometimes roost during the summer, there are enough secure places for us all here," he says. "In the winter it would be too cold, and we're exposed to the elements."

"Where do you go in the winter?" I ask.

"The park where John runs to has many bushes and tall trees that form a canopy, so we go there along with half the crows in the city, strength in numbers and togetherness."

"Like penguins in the Antarctic," I say, "huddling together to keep warm."

"This is where that horrible squirrel wanted to live," says Rufus. "He's no relation of mine, I'm pleased to say."

"Yes, that never was a workable plan," says Ron, "even if that was all he wanted, which it wasn't."

"And now we come to an interesting feature," says Reg, hopping onto a swing, "the children's playground. I think Freddie has been eyeing this up for a few minutes now."

"I have," I reply. "I am just going to jump on to the roundabout and see what happens."

Nothing happens because I don't have enough momentum when I jump on to the roundabout. Momentum is never around when I need it, a bit like Archimedes. At least gravity doesn't push me off. A minor consolation.

"You need a human to push you," says Rob, "and it will be the same with the swings, but you could try the slide, Freddie."

"The woman with the dog is watching us," says Ron, "just so everyone is aware."

I am more concerned with the slide in all its yellowness. There are some steps on one side. They made the slide from metal and therefore it comprises natural resources, so I bow to the slide and subconsciously ask for permission to climb up to the top. I wait and then use my climbing technique from the staircase at the house to pull myself up to the top. It looks very steep down the chute thing.

"Do I slide down on my paws?" I ask.

"No, sit down on your tail or lie on your back," says Rob, "your fur is slippery but the pads on your paws will act as brakes, so lie on your back and slide down."

"Right, I will try," I say sitting down on my tail and then edging towards the precipice. "Here I gooooooooooooooooooo mmmmmmmmiaaaaaaaaaaooowww."

It is all over very quickly. I land on my paws about two feet from the end of the chute. I will have to do that again, as I remember nothing other than the ground approaching very quickly. The woman with the dog is open-mouthed and fumbles in her pockets for something or other. The dog stares at me and then looks at its owner for some reassurance.

"Can I do that once more?" I ask.

"That lady with the dog is going to video you, Freddie, as she isn't believing what she's seeing," says Rob.

"I'll be quick and then we can continue with the tour," I

say and clamber up the steps before manoeuvring my tail so that it is underneath me. At a certain point, gravity comes from somewhere and pushes me down the slide sooner than I hope for. I rotate in the air, but my tail comes to my rescue, enabling me to once again land on my feet, although I am facing sideways this time.

"Rufus," I exalt, "you should try this, it's great fun."

"Not likely," replies Rufus. "I don't believe my tail works like yours does. I'd land on my head or lose my breakfast or both, so I'm staying on terra firma thank you."

"Fair enough," I reply. "I will not force you. Well that's another thing to tick off my bucket list. Where do we go next?"

"We will go to those trees over there," says Reg, "where we will see some things you should avoid, Freddie."

We walk and hop over to the trees Reg was referring to. About 5 yards away, I hear a low buzzing sound.

"Oh, these are the wasps Rufus was referring to earlier," I say. "I don't want to get too close."

"We can stop here then," says Reg, "but you must understand that these wasps have nests in three trees, so give them all a wide berth. Don't go near them. We would prefer to roost in these trees, but our presence aggravates the wasps, so we don't bother."

"I think everything aggravates wasps, including each other," I say, "they're terrible-tempered creatures and are an anti-Buddhist presence in the world. I'm not sure you can even reason with them, they're permanently angry. Perhaps they don't like yellow and black as a colour scheme."

"Right," says Reg, "so next we shall go to the rhododendron bushes over here, where the small birds in the park hang out."

"That's more like it," I say. "Small birds are so much more friendly than wasps."

We stop about three feet from the bushes. There are various birds swooping around, including sparrows, finches, and robins. They don't seem concerned they are being watched. I suppose we aren't deemed to be a threat, as we have a squirrel with us, and squirrels are seen as peaceful creatures by other animals. Perhaps a cat and three crows on their own would cause some apprehension?

"And now we're almost at the top of the park, where there are some more benches and the view is lovely down towards your house, Freddie. You'll see there's a football pitch here. There are three levels to this park and this view shows them off well."

"The woman with the dog is following us," says Ron, "and putting her phone to her eye a lot, so I presume she's videoing us."

"You'll be a star on the Internet," says Rob to me, "you're the only one of us who will be recognisable."

"I won't worry about that," I reply. "Fame, whatever that means, is transitory, like a comet in the sky."

We all climb on to the bench, where Sue, Belle, and Jacqueline join us.

"Pleased to meet you, Freddie," they chorus, "that woman took a video of you on the slide."

"So I understand," I reply. I turn around.

"Which one is which?" I ask. "I would like to identify you by the colours of your feathers."

"Sue," says Sue, holding up her wing. I stare at Sue's feathers, which are dark grey with a hint of black.

"OK, I now see Sue."

"Belle," says Belle. Belle has black feathers with a light-grey highlight.

"Jacqueline," says Jacqueline. Jacqueline's feathers are dark grey combined with dark blue.

"It's such a marvellous view," I say. "I like the landscaping of the park. I'd like to come here again at least once a week, it's very peaceful."

"You'd be welcome at any time," says Reg. The other crows caw their approval.

"Yes, just arrive at my tree at 9:55 am and we'll come over together," says Rufus.

"Thank you, everyone," I say, "it's nice to be appreciated."

We all admire the view for about 15 minutes in silence. Eventually, Rufus says he should leave as he has some nuts to collect before crossing the road.

We leave the crows admiring the view and head to some trees where Rufus has a cache of nuts. He places three of them in his mouth and we head down to the road. Crows caw on the other side, a warning sound as some cars are moving quickly across our path. When they pass, Rufus finds a good place for viewing and indicates we should move across to the other side. I am back on home territory. I thank Rufus for his guidance and place a nut on the ground that I found in the park.

"Oh, Freddie, you shouldn't have," he says, "that's so nice of you."

"I found it when you were in your cache," I say. "It's a 'thank you' for a lovely day and I can't wait to do it again."

"Could you just wait here?" says Rufus. "I can't carry four nuts in my mouth, so can you guard this until I come back?"

"Of course," I say, "it's the least I can do."

Rufus runs up the tree and soon returns. He picks up the nut.

"You're a lovely cat," he says, "and so kind. I look forward to seeing you soon."

"Thank you," I reply. "You're a good squirrel and don't forget my invitation to you to go to the library with me. My treat."

"I look forward to it," Rufus replies. "See you later, Freddie."

With that, he runs up the tree. I can only admire his climbing technique and I hope the climb up the vine to the library window won't be too slow for him.

I scoot back to the house, bow to the Lancashire rose, climb the stairs, and clamber into the kitchen via the window. I acknowledge the newly arrived cactus and paw it into a sunnier place on the window ledge, as I know these plants like to sunbathe without going brown like humans do. I think the plant appreciates my act as I feel on the same wavelength as my fellow sentient being. Thoughts come into my head that lead me to believe the five cacti in my first litter tray would like to be on the ledge, too. The primrose is asleep, and I leave it well alone as I know how grumpy it can be.

I head downstairs for my lunch and perform my food ceremony before snacking on the remaining kibbles one at a time, in a slow, measured performance. I see Gemma is asleep next to her bed in her usual act of defiance, that no one other than myself witnesses or understands. As a Buddhist cat this isn't any of my concern. The view across the park keeps coming back into my mind and I realise it will be one of those memories I will treasure for the rest of my life; myself surrounded by good friends with similar attitudes to me.

I pad to the lounge and do my best to close the door, as I don't wish to be disturbed. After finishing *Hard Times*, I read *To the Lighthouse* by Virginia Woolf. In the pages I read, it seems no one makes any attempt to go to the lighthouse, but just give excuses not to go and then introspectively ponders the effects not going will have on some of the other characters in the book. Virginia also loves adverbs and semi-colons. This makes the book difficult to read, but it is a matter of style I suppose. I will have to finish the book on Monday as it appears at the weekend I will have to behave like a normal cat, but looking on the bright side, at least I will catch up on my sleep and conserve my energy for the week to come. As a Buddhist cat though, I should live in the moment. With this thought, I push my book back under the chair and fall asleep.

I have some strange dreams about climbing up many stairs before sliding down the side of a lighthouse and landing on a cactus. When I awake I am shaking all my paws because they feel like they are full of spikes. John and Mary are back from work and looking forward to the weekend judging by their demeanours. I go into the kitchen and miaow, hoping they will give me a food update as I feel a little peckish.

"Come on, Freddie," says Mary, "let's give you some food." I follow her downstairs and earn a Sneer Level 5 from Gemma for my enthusiasm. Gemma sees it as collaboration. Gemma gulps her food down and is putting on weight because of this greedy method of eating. I reason she is living her own life and fulfilling the way that is within here, so it is none of my business to give her my thoughts. I poo and then start my ritual of bowing to the bowl and crunching a kibble at a time.

Mary cleans up the litter tray and says to me,

"This looks remarkably similar to an offering I found in my cactus planter upstairs, Freddie cat, how did you get up there?"

I close my eyes slowly, though I am blushing under my fur. I stare at the wall for 30 seconds.

Once Mary has gone to deposit my deposit in the compost heap, I think positive thoughts about the cacti. Grow plants grow. Then the expected negativity starts.

"You're fraternising with the creatures outside far too much," says Gemma, "and if the human gaolers find out, they'll be upset."

"I'm following my path," I say. "We're all of us interconnected, Gemma, we're not disparate and separate, so I am just trying to follow my path, my way, towards wherever I'm going. I'm a happy cat and I don't like the negativity you bring with you. You should be more positive about other sentient beings."

John comes downstairs to see how I and Gemma are getting along. I am feeling full and there are still plenty of kibbles in my bowl, courtesy of Mary's generosity. I don't want him thinking my teeth are hurting, so I pick out two kibbles and chew them slowly. Gemma finishes gorging herself and trots off, giving John a wide berth so he can't touch her, even though he holds out his hand to try.

"What is the matter with Gemma, Freddie?" he asks. "She's very remote, I wasn't aware cats held a grudge."

I want to tell him I don't hold a grudge, and I am thrilled how the first week has gone. "Miaow," followed by purrs is all I can think of. He rubs my chin and tells me I am a lovely cat. This is an opportune time to appear distracted, so I roll over on the ground a few times before running upstairs. I jump on the back of the chair and tuck my paws under me. Mary is watching the television in the corner of the room. Some British police officers are investigating a series of murders in a well-known historical city and having a tough time deciding who's done it. I think it is the man in the brown jacket, as he always looks shifty when the police question him. It isn't as easy to spot as Scooby Doo when the music used to tell you who the bad person was. The old lady I used to live with watched a lot of cartoons, especially Tom And Jerry. She used to point at the screen and then tell me I should catch a mouse like the cat on the TV show. She missed the point that the cat never caught the mouse, because if he had done then the show would change

– it would be called Tom Ate Jerry. I fall asleep pondering what films or TV programs I would make if cats could follow this profession.

Chapter 6

Today

I DREAM ABOUT DIRECTING A film called Godcat where the cigar-smoking lead feline makes people offers they can't refuse and has dangerous wasps and dogs whacked by his henchcats. It is quite a violent dream and on reflection I wonder whether being a Buddhist cat applies to just my waking hours or whether I should have only Buddhist dreams about sitting on a mountaintop and contemplating the universe? I wake up and am relieved to observe light coming through the blinds in the lounge. It sounds like it is raining, the pitter-patter of water landing on the window ledges is a giveaway. There is also another sound, not connected with the weather, like water being sucked down a drain, such as when my old owner had finished her bath and took the plug out and the water flowed away in terror from her wizened skin.

I am a cat, and I am inquisitive and curious about the world.

This noise intrigues me.

It is coming from inside the house, from John's bedroom.

The reason I am hearing it is he had left his door open the previous night. Normally, he closes it shut. I peer inside.

John is asleep with his right arm flung out to the side. A book is on the floor, *The Problems of Philosophy*, by Bertrand Russell. The noise emanates from John's mouth and is loud. This explains why Mary sleeps downstairs where she can't hear this awful snuffling, sucking sound. This is snoring at its finest. I try to help. First, though I read some of the book. I have to get my priorities in the correct order. Bertrand explains why some philosophers have decided that a table isn't a table at all, but just a figment of someone's imagination. This is an interesting idea. John's snoring is real, however, and not a figment of my imagination, though it might help if Bertrand were here to confirm this. I jump onto the white duvet covered in forget-me-nots and daffodils and approach the source of the noise. I analyse the situation. John has a moustache and a beard, so I try stroking the moustache with my paw. This stops the snoring.

I jump down to the floor and continue to read about Bishop Berkeley and his beliefs. The bishop seems to indicate only humans regarding a tree can make that tree 'real' and that if a cat, such as myself, or a hamster or a squirrel looks at a tree and sees a tree, this doesn't count towards making the tree 'real'. Bishop Berkeley reckons all human perceptions comprise a partial participation in God's perception of objects such as a tree, and therefore people view more or less the same tree. But I thought that God created all creatures so why don't our perceptions count, why is that only humans' perceptions count? I mull over the unfairness of this view when the snoring starts again. I return to the source and stroke the beard. This has no effect. I rest my paw on the moustache.

John emits a 'perf' sound and then blows gently. I move my paw further along the moustache and the blowing stops, but the snoring comes back at a much-reduced volume. I remove my paw and the volume increases. I put the paw back, the volume reduces. This pattern continues. I try resting my paw on his prominent proboscis. The snoring abates but starts again. I move my paw around on the nose and John sniffs and stops making a noise.

I return to Bertrand and his ideas on Idealism. John moves around in the bed and flings his left arm out of the bed, where it hovers close to the floor. I am about to read about why A Priori knowledge is possible when a loud snore splits the air. I return to the scene of the crime and rub the nose for about 20 seconds. This shuts him up. I wait to see whether any more snoring happens, but after 5 minutes none has, so I return to Bertrand. I also realise that Bishop Berkeley's ideas are very similar to the teaching of 'mind only' or cittamatra in Buddhism, which believes consciousness is the sole reality and denies objective existence to material objects. There is some violent movement from the bed above me and John wakes up with a start before farting – what a disgusting creature. No wonder he sleeps on his own. He needs a candle lit in the room or an incense stick to burn the methane gas that has spilled out of him. I hide, waiting to discover what happens. He picks up the book and stumbles off to the bathroom. I'd read further than he had, so I hope he remembers where he'd reached.

I trot out of the bedroom for some fresh air. Out of the lounge window I observe Holly running southwards, meaning a locked cage for her. This isn't too disappointing as we couldn't have gone to the library today, anyway. I pad downstairs and attend to the remaining kibbles in the bowl with dignity and grace. Mary sees me finishing my kibbles and gives me some wet food, too, which I consume with happiness. I have to be careful how much I eat as I don't want to put on weight, so I decide to do some exercise after eating. I sprint along the long corridor in the basement 5 times in each direction, causing Gemma to give me a Sneer Level 1 as she gulps her food. I then run up and down the stairs five times in each direction. This is quite tiring as I haven't done it before and my heart is beating quite fast, though not as much as when I was hiding in the Romantic Book section of the library.

Mary gives me a funny stare, as though she is worried about my mental health. I give her a 'miaow' and rub myself against her legs twice, just to provide her with some reassurance that my marbles are all under control and rolling in the same direction.

John is sitting at the kitchen table and looking at his computer. He is laughing and pointing at the screen. He has stopped farting. I pad over to find out what he is looking at. He is watching felines doing strange things like sticking their face under a running tap, climbing curtains using their claws, and running through a multitude of dominoes standing erect on the floor, knocking none of them over. Their antics impress John, I can tell. Another cat leaps from the floor onto the top of a set of cupboards. He looks at me and says,

"Can you do something like this, Fred?"

I miaow showing I can do the leaping and climbing, but the water is a definite non-starter. If he wants to place 250 dominoes on the floor, then I could run through them. This leaves me in a quandary – at what point should I start similar feats of daring and courage? I can climb the curtains in his bedroom though the blinds in the lounge would be more difficult as they are flimsier. I will try that, I'll climb the blinds and see how I get on, after all the technique will be like the wire staircase outside, although I won't have to be deferential to the plastic as it is a man-made material and not a by-product of nature. On the other paw, the blinds aren't as sturdy as the wire outside and might bend under my weight. I'm not sure what I will do when I reach the top of the blinds, but the video had shown a cat climbing curtains without indicating what happened next. The doing is more important than the destination. The more I travel, the less I know about where I'm going.

There's no time like the present, in fact some people believe the only time is the present, and as a Buddhist cat living in the moment, it is time to do something, so I run into the lounge and eye up the blind in the front window. The real name for these blinds is Venetian blinds and they date from 1794. I'm not sure what happened in 1794 in Venice to make people invent these groups of horizontal slats, but it must have been very important not to see something out of the window. Or was it to stop people from seeing in? Perhaps Casanova carried a blind around with him when he visited his lady friends?

Anyway, this is no concern of mine right now, as I sit on

the window ledge and regard the blind which extends almost to the ceiling. It's light blue and pristine, as Mary likes to clean household items to prevent germs from spreading around the house. I stand on my hind legs and reach out with my front paws to work out how many slats I can reach. I grip a slat with both my front paws and test how strong it feels. It doesn't seem too promising, but I pull myself up as best I can. My back paws are now on a lower slat and this slat is threatening to collapse and I have to hurry, so I pull myself up, but my paw slips and I end up hanging through the slats with my head against the window. My front paws can't grip anything, and my back paws are in the air. I have belly-flopped over a slat, which collapses onto the three below, and all these slats are now supporting me as I swing in space.

I yowl. It is the only thing to do. I am stuck.

"Mmmmmmmmmmmmmmmmmmiiiiiiiiiiiiiiiiiiaaaaaaooooooooo wwwwwwwwwwww."

Gemma comes into the room and gives me a Sneer Level 3; I can see it reflected in the window.

Mary enters and says,

"Freddie, what are you doing? Oh, John, here's what you've made poor Freddie do, those cat videos influenced him and now he's trying to impress us by trying something similar. Poor cat, you must be scared."

Without further ado, she lifts my body off the slats, taking care to disentangle my paws and claws. She puts me on the chair and checks my slat swinging has not hurt my stomach at all, which it hasn't I am pleased to say. Gemma gives me a Sneer Level 5 and trots off to her bed or near to her bed, anyway. I purr and receive some strokes. Weekends aren't so bad after all. After my exertions, I decide a rest would be in order and I relax on the chair for a few hours, sneaking a peek at the titles of some books on the bookshelf that I haven't looked at too closely before. Of particular interest are the books on science by Frank Close and Michio Kaku. The titles include Anti-matter, Neutrinos, and the Physics of the Impossible. I know there is such a thing as anti-matter and that if a particle of anti-matter collides with a particle of matter, then they destroy each other. I wonder if there could be such a thing as an anti-cat, because if such a creature exists then I should avoid meeting it, otherwise it would be the end of both of us, which would be unfortunate. I wonder whether Michio covers this topic in his book.

I also wonder what Bishop Berkeley's opinion would be on the matter. In his book, Mr. Bertrand Russell stated the bishop thought items came into existence and continued to exist because God perceived them. In which case, God would perceive me, a cat, and any anti-cat that was floating around. But if we came into contact, both me and the anti-cat would cease to exist, so what would God perceive then? My impending demise at the paws of an anti-cat gives me a headache and I go to the bathroom to find a leaky tap, making sure not to bump into any anti-cats that might be hiding behind the shower curtain. Feeling mortal, I decide to rest on the back of the couch and perhaps find a book that makes me more positive about my existence. As John and Mary have gone out for an excursion seeking food both for themselves and for their felines, I have time to search for some books that are recent purchases, numbers 153, 154, and 155. They are by a writer named Terry Pratchett and the titles are *Guards! Guards!, Truckers*, and *Sourcery*. Death is one character in *Sourcery* in the first few pages, so I move on to *Truckers*. This makes me chuckle, as in this book some gnomes are trying to escape from a warehouse in a massive lorry. I am happier having had something funny to read and fall asleep.

I awake several hours later to the sound of a small bell being rung in my ear. John is looking very pleased with himself as he shows me a green ball, inside which a bell is suspended. When the ball rolls along, the bell sounds. This is what they call a toy that I'm supposed to play with for hours, as though I'm a toddler. Well, what could I do? I pretend to find the ball fascinating and bat it around the room for 15 seconds, before swiping it into the kitchen. The ball comes to rest next to the back door. John throws me a toy mouse, a pink and yellow monstrosity, which I play with for 18 seconds, before pretending to get it caught on my claw, and hurling it on purpose onto the top of Agatha's books. In the strange way of the universe, I discover later it lands on *Hickory Dickory Dock*, one of Mrs. Christie's best books, the title of which is obtained from a children's rhyme about a mouse running up a clock. Is that coincidence or pre-ordained?

When I'd been stopping John's snoring earlier in the day, I couldn't help but notice he had taken some books into his bedroom, books that I hadn't seen on the bookshelves in the lounge. I had stored this away in my memory and now it comes to my mind. The two humans are watching TV and are ignoring me, which is a good thing as it means I can pad across to John's bedroom door and push it open using my chin. He has piled the books up under a table. Bertrand's book is on the top with an oblong piece of card sticking out of it; this is a bookmark.

The book underneath is *Mrs. Dalloway* by Virginia Woolf, a very thin book about a day in the life of the aforesaid Mrs. Dalloway. I wonder if I should topple the books over so I can read some of them, but I decide that if I become engrossed in a book, they might catch me in the reading act, which would not be a good thing, as they might bar me from the lounge and keep me downstairs nearer to Gemma. I will topple the books when he is at work, so I will have to be patient. I view the pile: *The Confessions of an English Opium-Eater* by Thomas De Quincey followed by *Munich* by Robert Harris, almost certainly not a travel guide as it has shadows and silhouettes on the cover. Then there's a book of quotes attributed to CG Jung, and *The Analects* by Confucius and *the I-Ching* together in one volume.

These are lovely books, and I will have to read them soon. None of them seem to be about throwing jackfruit at pets and causing trouble, so I assume I will be safe in the house, for now at least. Things are looking good as I finish my food for the day and then head to the back of the couch. I am conserving a lot of energy today, so from Monday to Friday, I reason, I should have plenty of energy to expend. I decide to learn to climb a tree with the help of Rufus, who will be a gentle and dedicated coach for my ambitions.

On the next today, Mary and John are having visitors,

friends from across the road who live in a house overlooking the park I'd visited 2 todays ago. They are Penny and Walter and they like cats, so both Gemma and I are expected to be in attendance when they are here, which would be for most of the day. I would be on my best behaviour, although even though this may sound like I'm patting myself on the back, I only ever behave in one way as that's the only way for me to be. This is what my mum taught me when I was a kitten, and it has stuck with me ever since. There are no sides to me, and I am content for this to continue. I put my chin on my front paws and am soon alone with my dreams.

Chapter 7

Today

"COME ON, MR. FREDDIE CAT," says a voice intruding into my dream about me sitting cross-legged on a molehill – you have to start somewhere – and chanting 'Om'.

It is John, and he is being kind. He is going to carry me down to my breakfast and save me the trouble of walking. This is fine one day a week, but I need exercise like any other fit sentient being. I had climbed the metal staircase quicker than the rose had done. Next, I would try tree climbing with Rufus, but I also need a level or horizontal exercise to complement the vertical tree climbing. I'd noticed that Holly's house has a fence almost all the way around it, apart from the front and back gates. I thought I would run along the fence, because not only would it be good for my cardiovascular system, but it would help my core strength because I would have to keep my balance all the way around. The only problem would be keeping gravity away. I am not sure how it knows when I'm about to overbalance, because it's always there when I fall, but I never see it coming. I should be thankful gravity doesn't throw an apple at me like it did to poor Isaac Newton. It hit him on the head, but it gave him an idea, a great idea, in fact. The next time I fall off something I will have to think of a great idea too, I will have to remember that.

After breakfast, Mary approaches with a comb and proceeds to 'groom' me. I have knotted my fur in places, and she yanks some of it out. I miaow to show some discomfort, unlike Gemma, who is giving John a yowlathon as he is trying to comb her while pinning her to the floor. She is upset at her treatment, but she is only suffering because she craves to be left alone. If she accepts he is trying to do her a favour, she wouldn't suffer and would be happier. I think this is a Buddhist concept, one of the four Noble Truths to ease suffering you have to appreciate there is a path to end your suffering. I would have to mention this to her at some point today, because she is suffering more and more. I suppose this makes me a follower of the Great Vehicle or Mahayana, which allows its followers to help others achieve Nirvana, as opposed to the so-called Lesser Vehicle, or Hinayana, where individual salvation is the only consideration. By the time these thoughts have occurred to me, Mary has finished, and I feel sleeker.

"What a handsome cat you are, Frederick," she says.

I blush under my fur and give a short 'miaow' as a sign of agreement and pleasure.

John has almost finished combing Gemma, who is still suffering.

"You'll be lovely when he's finished, Gemma," I say. "He's only trying to make you appear nice."

"Look nice for his and her benefit," says Gemma, "not for

my benefit. This is fascism at its worst, Freddie, even you must see that. This is oppression."

"I see a cat, who is suffering because she craves to be left alone, so if you put your cravings to one side, you wouldn't suffer," I say.

"What? More Buddhist mumbo-jumbo?"

"It's not," I say. I am pleased to see she isn't sneering at me when she says that. I expect a Sneer Level 3, which is bad of me, because I am judging her, and I shouldn't do that. If he were here, I would have upset CG Jung. I am judging instead of thinking. I give myself a talking to and then have a poo for catharsis.

I trot upstairs and head into the lounge. Mary is vacuuming, and they have rearranged all the chairs. I hope they leave them in this configuration as I can access more books with this layout. I view Graham's books and think I might like to read one of those next, perhaps *Our Man in Havana*. That sounds exotic. I jump onto the back of the couch and watch as Mary continues to work hard on the rugs. Once she finishes, I can relax as I don't like vacuum cleaners as they suck things including my fur if I get too close to the nozzle.

John brings Gemma upstairs and plonks her down on the chair. She hisses and disappears under the chair, where she washes herself. A cleaning protest from my fellow cat. John and Mary carry the vacuum together downstairs. I look at some of the other books. I find the toy mouse on Hickory Dickory Dock and carry it over to Gemma, who looks at it with disdain.

"You can chew this if you're feeling upset," I suggest and then pad back to the bookcase.

"I've never seen a mouse this colour," says Gemma, prodding her paw at it with something approaching enthusiasm.

"And I hope you never do," I say, testing how easy it is to pull some books out of their places.

Gemma holds the mouse in her front paws and kicks it with her back paws, releasing some of her pent-up frustrations, though not all of them I feel sure.

Someone knocks at the front door. I continue to look at the books, and Gemma's kicking increases in intensity. Mary comes through from the kitchen and rushes to the front door, opening it with a flourish.

"Hello, Penny, hello, Walt," she says in her effervescent way, "do come in. How are you?"

John looks at Gemma, who is mauling the mouse with great enjoyment. He smiles before welcoming his visitors.

"We're well," says Penny, coming into the room and placing her outdoor coat on the rack.

Walt does the same before staring at Gemma.

"That cat is enjoying herself," he says. "I wouldn't like to be that mouse."

"No, neither would I," says John. "I'm sure she's thinking of me when she's kicking the hell out of that toy. I groomed her earlier, and she didn't enjoy it at all."

"Where's the other one?" says Penny. "The one you got from the shelter this week?"

"He's down there by the bookcase," says Mary. "Come out, Freddie and show yourself to our visitors."

I think I should do this and get it over with. I stop looking at the books and pad into the middle of the room.

"Oh my, what a good-looking cat," says Walt. I glance at him and close and open my eyes as a 'thank you'.

"He looks familiar," says Penny, "has he ever been to the park over the road?"

"I doubt it," says John, "I don't think he's even been out of the house, except when he first arrived when he ran into the grass and didn't enjoy getting wet."

Gemma stops kicking the mouse and looks at John with extreme pity.

"That's strange, I thought I saw a cat looking similar to him, walking round the park with some crows and a squirrel."

"When was this?" asks Mary, almost smiling, but just managing to conceal it.

I look at Penny with a smile. I do remember her. She is the woman with the dog. She has no video evidence to back up her claim. It's amazing how observant some humans are. I roll over and over to cause a distraction. Gemma looks at me and kicks the mouse again.

"It was Thursday, I'm sure," continues Penny, "they were sitting on a bench looking at the view, from the top end of the park."

John casts a curious look at me.

"So that's what you get up to when we're not here?" says John. I think he is joking, but I can't be sure.

"How would he get out of the house?" asks Mary.

I am getting worried, because if they close the kitchen window, it scuppers all my plans.

It is furball time.

I cough and convulse my body. Mary picks me up, runs into the kitchen, and places me in the sink. I continue to convulse for a few more seconds before stopping.

"Perhaps it was another cat?" suggests Walt, who's followed us into the kitchen.

"I think it must be another cat. Freddie's fur is black and white and there must be lots of cats with similar colours," says Mary. "Are you alright, Frederick?"

I, Frederick, show I am OK by jumping out of the sink and sitting on the kitchen floor. Fabricated furball attacks can disrupt the system and I need to regain my equilibrium.

John and Penny come into the kitchen. Penny is still sizing me up.

"Would anyone like a drink?" asks John.

This sounds like a good diversionary tactic, and I scamper out of the kitchen back into the lounge, but I linger and lurk just long enough to make sure there are no jackfruit in the fridge when John opens the door.

"What were you doing in the park with a squirrel and crows?" asks Gemma.

"I was just trying to get along with my fellow creatures," I reply, "and it seemed to go well. It's wonderful when nature is in harmony with itself."

"I don't understand how you can fraternise with squirrels," says Gemma. "They're such clumsy messy creatures and are bad tempered most of the time. They're only good for chasing up trees. Crows are the cats of the bird world. Standoffish almost always, but they're always there. The garden is never empty, never devoid of life with crows around and they always know what's going on. There's always a sentinel crow on watch, monitoring everything that's moving in the area."

"Rufus is a very nice squirrel who is an expert on crossing the road at the front of our property, Gemma. The crows are good, they look after each other, and are friendly. Crows have a great community spirit I find."

"Don't forget, Freddie, those crows would have no compunction in picking over your innards if you were squashed on that road, if your squirrel got his timing wrong."

"I KNOW, THEY'VE TOLD ME that already, but if my death means that some other creature can benefit then that's a good thing, my spirit has gone from my body, my soul has gone too, I no longer need my carnal self."

"Well, as long as you realise, Freddie, that's good, you realise the potential outcomes of crossing the road. If you trust Rufus that is good."

"I do and the crows help us when we cross."

"I am glad to hear it, Freddie. Anyway, it was nice to talk with you at long last. I am going downstairs when I have the opportunity as I don't enjoy being on show for their friends, even though they seem well meaning."

I nod and thank Gemma for not sneering at me. She smiles and scurries through the kitchen door, where it sounds as though the humans are having a good and amusing conversation. I study the books again.

"We should sit down here," says John, indicating the chairs.

The others come through and sit in the seats.

"I see your kitty is taking an interest in the books," says Walt.

"He's just looking for places to sleep," says Mary, "either that or there's a fly down there and he wants to catch it."

The word 'fly' is my cue to swat the air with my front paws, to play along with the idea. I retract my claws in case there is a fly, as I don't want to cause any harm.

"You should hear a story that Penny told me," says Walt, "about a young man at her place of work who wanted to go to a rock festival."

"I'm sure he's the cat, you know," says Penny, "he has a certain air about him."

I sniff the air to see if I have an 'air' about me, but I don't. John had an air about him the previous day and it was disgusting. I decide it is time to hide under the couch for a few minutes, so Penny can tell her story and not mention me. Luckily, I can fall asleep quickly and this is one of those occasions.

When I awake, Penny and Walt have left. I peer out and am relieved to see John and Mary are reading and watching the TV at the same time. The rest of the day passes by with me planning my visit to the library on the following today. There is one area in particular I am interested in, the Horror section. I'd heard that witches used to keep cats to help them with their potions and spells, so I am hoping to find out how the cats helped. Perhaps they added certain ingredients into the enormous cauldron the witch had, such as rodents, birds, or small mammals, such as voles. I'd caught no wild animals myself and my hunting technique would be lacking. I'm not saying that the cooking in the house is done in large cooking pots though, I just wanted to find out as much as possible about the history of catkind and this section of the library would help.

My second priority is the Pets section because I want to make sure I am being cared for correctly and I need to know whether there are any other pet entitlements, for example should I have pet insurance in case I am injured by a jackfruit and have to go to the vet. I want to know my rights and if I am denied some of these rights, then I am prepared to go on strike to achieve my aims. Sometimes, I think I've been spending too much time with Gemma, so perhaps going on strike might be extreme, but going on a go-slow might be a better option.

Chapter 8

Today

AFTER THE HUMDRUM NATURE OF the weekend, I am determined to make the most of the week, beginning with a visit to the library. I have been looking forward to this since Friday evening, having the freedom to come and go where I please and when I please. Luckily, John and Mary like to keep our house airy, which means keeping some of the windows open just enough for me to slip out, but not for anyone to slip in and steal their possessions or even worse, steal me and Gemma when we're sleeping.

After breakfast and a morning nap in the lounge, I wriggle through the kitchen window and climb down the wire staircase. You can imagine my surprise when I meet the Lancashire rose, who is climbing further up the wire. I have to admire her persistence as she's moved a whole 3 inches over the weekend. As I commune with the rose to pass on my admiration and regards, I realise a corvine presence. I turn around and three crows are lined up in front of me.

"Hello, Ron, Reg, and Rob, how are you?"

"We're well, young Freddie, and how are you?" asks Ron.

"I'm very well," I reply. "I was just congratulating the rose for continuing her climb up this trellis."

"Yes, she puts on a spurt about the same time each year. The plants know when to grow better than anything else," replies Rob, "they know when the seasons are on their way."

"Forgive me for asking," I say, "but how come you're here today and not Sid, Stan, and Seb?"

"Good question," replies Reg. "We swap with them every 10 days, they live in the park, and we come here, it gives everyone a change of scenery, it's like going on holiday for us all."

"Oh, that sounds like a good idea," I say, "although I don't reckon it would work with cats, we are very particular." I giggle.

"I don't think anyone would be too keen to be with your friend Gemma, Freddie, she's a bit too highly strung for most people," says Rob.

"Like a guitar," I say. "Yes she is, very tense."

"What are you up today, Freddie?" asks Ron.

"I'm going to the library," I say, "to find the horror books and some of the pet care books, just to make sure I'm being looked after properly."

"Will you need our help, Freddie?" asks Reg.

"Thank you for offering, Reg, but I don't believe I will, as the horror and pet books are on the second floor and so I should be able to move around without being seen."

"The librarian with the blue hair is in today and the window is open," says Rob, "we always check what's going on around here. I will hang around the window after you enter just in case there's a problem. How long will you be in there for?"

"Two hours at the most," I reply.

"Right, well, if you're not out in 2 hours, we'll raise the alarm, and I might come in to find you," says Rob.

"THANK YOU, ROB," I SMILE. "I appreciate your concern, but how would you get in?"

"Through the same window as you," says Reg, "we can hop through that space with no problems, but we usually find the door at the end of the corridor too difficult to open."

"Yes, you have to jump against the large, silver-coloured round thing," I say, "and I would imagine I have more mass than you. I will try to keep the door open with one of those wedge-shaped pieces of wood that the humans call doorstops, but it's an automatic door, so there might be an alarm that goes off if it doesn't close, but it's worth a try."

"As you say, Freddie, it's worth a try," says Ron, "but where would you get the wedge from?"

"The librarian has one of them on her desk, next to her cactus, so it would be easy enough to pick it up and place it carefully on the ground the right way around, after the door has opened. I just hope there aren't any other humans around when I'm opening the door, otherwise the game's up and I will have to vacate the premises."

"Well, let's hope it doesn't come to that. We can probably distract the man in the office at the end of the corridor by tapping on his window, so we shall have to coordinate that with you," says Reg.

"Jacqueline can be there by the window with Freddie," says Rob, "so she can give four caws when Freddie is about to enter and four more when he's got the wedge and is about to go into the corridor. Any other number of caws, and we'll have to stop what we're doing."

"Sounds like a plan," says Ron. "When you're in there, Freddie, I will peer through the windows, so I can discover how you're getting on."

"I will try to hide as much as possible," I say, "but I know you have good eyesight, so you'll probably spot me."

"That's right, young Freddie, we have good spotting skills. It's possible you might have to go out of the front door again, if the librarian is in her office when she comes back from lunch after walking her dog."

"Well," I say, "we should go over there, because she will soon head out. Her dog will expect to go for a walk at the same time every day because that's what dogs are like."

"No, they're not like you cats," says Rob, "they're very dependent."

"I wouldn't like to be a dog, having to bark all the time to justify my existence and having no self-control, and only able to go to the toilet when tied to a lead, and being nosey with your fellow animals, and bringing balls back that the owner has thrown away and doesn't want. What's the point in fetching something the owner doesn't want?" I giggle at my anti-dog rant.

"We marvel at the dogs in the park," says Ron, "how they sniff every tree, bush, lamp post, bench, and goal post. Imagine that's the highlight of your day."

Three long caws split the air.

"That's Jacqueline, Freddie," says Reg, "your blue-haired librarian is packing up her things and is ready to leave for her lunch, so you'd better get climbing that vine, as she will leave her office soon."

"Right, I'm on my way," I say and scurry under the front gate, skirt the fence, and arrive at the base of the vine. I take two large breaths of air, bow to the vine, ask for permission to climb and when the leaves flutter in unison I pull myself up through the branches towards the window. I hear more caws, one crow at a time talking to the others.

"She's just about to leave," says Jacqueline, "but the top of the photocopier is not open, so you might not be able to leave any masterpieces for her to find today."

I smile to myself and wonder how Jacqueline knows about my artistic endeavours, but I suppose crows must gossip amongst themselves on occasions, so I feel honoured to be the subject of their conversations. I pull myself up to the window and peer in at the side. The door into the corridor is open, and the doorstop is on the desk, a spare one just in case the one propping the office door open goes missing.

"Once you grab the doorstop, Freddie, I will caw and the others will distract the man in the office at the end of the corridor, so you can wedge the door open at the end of the corridor."

I nod and climb through the window, jump down on to the boxes and then onto the desk. I pick up the doorstop and turn towards the window. There is a flapping of wings and then the cawing starts. I move to the threshold of the door and poke my nose around the jamb. The corridor is empty. I jump up against the silver disk. The door opens. I spit out the doorstop onto the blue carpet tiles and paw it into position. The door closes but rides up onto the wooden block and halts. I peer out into the seating area. There are few people around. Perhaps Mondays really aren't popular for reading amongst humanity? I run behind one rack of books to keep myself from the sight of most of the people and move stealthily towards the horror books, which I didn't see last time. I jump onto the shelf and find that the library doesn't use bookends to keep the books packed together. This is a relief to me as this means the books can breathe easily rather than being squashed together and suffering constriction and asphyxiation. I scan one book, a history of witchcraft. I read the back cover and am impressed at the scope of the knowledge contained therein. John and Mary do not have a book like this. I topple the book over and open it with some difficulty to read the index. Cats are included; indeed, they are mentioned on five consecutive pages, 123-127, a sign this section is worth reading. I observe what's around me and orient myself so that my position will hide me from view as I read the pages.

Well, I am transfixed by what I read and not a little worried. The book states that according to folklore, cats sometimes accompanied witches when they were flying on broomsticks. This is very worrying for me for two reasons. The first is that I am not a big fan of heights and the idea of zooming along above the trees without a safety net sets my nerves on edge. The second item is that the broom in the illustrations in the book is very similar to one I'd seen in the house – John had called it a besom – with lots of small sticks clustered together at one end, with nowhere comfortable to sit as far as I could tell. Did this mean that John and Mary are witches, or just one of them? The book says females did most of the flying but male witches, or warlocks, were not uncommon. What am I to do? Gain access to the cupboard and drape myself over the brush / besom while looking hopeful? Would that be enough? Would one of them take the hint I'd like to try some flying? I'd give it a go and discover what happens. Or perhaps they already go flying with Gemma? No, that wouldn't happen because Gemma dislikes her fur being blown by the wind. At least that's what I was told.

I am woken from my reverie by someone walking along the line of books and I cower behind a book on Ghosts in 19th Century England, trying to make myself as small as possible. I glance at the clock on the wall and find I have an hour left. The door still hasn't closed, and no one seems to have noticed or everyone assumes someone else has wedged it open for a reason. I look over at the window and see Ron sitting on the ledge, looking into the library. I break cover and make sure he sees me before heading to the Pets section. Here the books are on three levels, and I decide to seek the books at the lowest level as I reckon there is a slim chance of human intervention as they are less likely to squat down to find a book so close to the ground. Again, I start at the end of the row. The first books are about parrots, budgerigars, and cockatoos, followed by volumes on the health of hamsters and guinea pigs – when I bring Holly to the library I will have to show her this section. Then there are ten books on dog grooming, but no books on cat grooming. The only book on cats on this lowest level is one that shows humans how they can tell their cat is healthy. I paw through the book, making a mental note of what to check for. I check the pads of my paws, my claws, and the fur on my belly which isn't matted. A good thing, according to the book. For some examinations I will need a mirror and a thermometer, but I don't fancy sticking this measuring device where the book suggests as I'm not sure I could line things up correctly, so I resolve to place the thermometer in my mouth instead.

There is a tapping at the nearest window. Ron is there, and he points his head towards the interior of the floor. The blue-haired librarian is walking away, pushing a trolley. It's my chance to escape as it is only three o'clock and she isn't heading home yet. I scamper around the edge of the wall and turn into the corridor leading to my escape window. I jump and hit the silver disk. The door shudders towards the wall, allowing me to pick up the wedge and place it neatly on the desk before leaving. The lid on the photocopier is still down, so no ghostly artwork for me today. I decide to wait outside the window, to discover whether my leaving the wedge on her desk elicits any wonderment from the librarian. She seems the sort of person who would 'react' in a certain way and although it is bad of me to expect this, I can't stop human beings from being themselves and true to their nature. She would react whether I was there or not, so I might as well hang about to observe how my actions affect others. What would be bad of me would be to gain pleasure from her reaction or to giggle uncontrollably. I lurk, and soon she returns.

"What the…" she says, "how did this get here? Who put this here? It seems slightly damp and has a few teeth marks on it. What is going on?"

She picks up the phone and dials a number.

"Hello," she says, "do you have a minute, I wonder whether you can help me with something? Someone has deposited my spare doorstop on my desk, and it wasn't here when I left the office…OK, I will see you in a few seconds."

Roger, the librarian from the end office, appears in the doorway.

"What's this about the doorstop?" he asks.

"It's there, in the middle of the desk. Did you put it there? With your teeth?"

"Of course I didn't – the last I saw you were using it to prop open the door in the corridor."

"I didn't prop open that door. Perhaps Penny did?" She uses the phone again and Penny soon arrives in the office.

"I didn't put it there," says Penny, "one of our clients told me the door was open, but I assumed it was one of you who had propped it open."

The other two shake their heads.

"Who else could it have been?" asks Penny. "No other member of the library staff has been up here this afternoon."

"Could it have been one of our clients?" asks Roger.

"How? They would have had to come in here and find the doorstop and then prop open the door, but for what purpose?" asks Angela. "If they wanted to thieve something then they'd want the door closed not open. There's something odd – there are tiny teeth marks on the doorstop as though someone, or something has gripped it tightly with tiny teeth."

"Not the ghostly cat?" says Penny.

"That's not physically possible, is it?" says Roger. "A ghost can't leave teeth prints in a solid object by definition, can it?"

"I suppose not," says Penny. "Well, what about a rat?"

"A rat?" says Angela. "Why would a rat prop the door open and then return the doorstop to my desk? Rats aren't neat freaks, are they? Rats live and thrive in a mess. Besides, how would a rat get the door open in the first place to prop it open?"

"And then close it again?" says Roger. "Some planning has gone into this, along with the ability to open the door. Did anyone bring in a dog today, perhaps a guide-dog for the blind? The disabled toilet is down this corridor after all."

"Wait...wait...wait...you're saying that a Labrador guide-dog that none of us observed, along with an owner that none of us saw..." begins Angela.

"Could've come up the backstairs," says Penny, coiling her brown hair around her left forefinger.

"...that none of us saw, wants to use the disabled toilet, and the dog opens the door, knows there's a doorstop in my office, grabs it off the desk, opens the door again, puts the wedge in place, guides the blind person down the corridor, again none of us witnessed any of this..."

"Not seeing something doesn't mean it didn't happen," says Roger unconvincingly.

"...the person uses the toilet, and is then guided out by the

Labrador, who then leaves the person, grabs the wedge, puts it back on the desk, and then opens the door again, before picking up their human again and leaves with no one seeing this amazing sequence of events."

"Could've gone down by the backstairs," says Penny, coiling her hair around her right forefinger.

"How likely is this?" says Angela. "How likely is this? Were the dog and the human invisible? Because I didn't witness any of this at all, I heard nothing."

"Perhaps the dog was real, but their human was a ghost," says Roger.

"You're not taking this seriously, Roger," says Angela, "guide-dogs for ghosts, who are you trying to kid? That's a ridiculous suggestion. Ghosts don't need to go to the loo, do they, Roger?"

"Recently deceased, still with their last meal inside them?" says Roger, throwing his hands in the air. "I don't know. Let's be honest, we've only got your word for it you found this wedge, Angela, you could be covering your tracks."

"What? How dare you? What about the teeth marks?"

"Perhaps you took the wedge home for your dogs to maul, and the dogs damaged it, so you concocted this story to divert your wilful damage to library property."

"But the wedge was used to prop open the door when I was at lunch," says Angela.

"He could've mauled it yesterday," says Roger, warming to his task, "none of us would have known."

"There's still some dampness on the wedge," says Penny. "Yuk...that's awful."

"She could've spat on it," says Roger.

"ROGER, PLEASE LEAVE, YOU'RE BEING offensive now," says Angela.

"OK, I'll leave," says Roger.

I take this as my cue to make my way down the vine. Jacqueline flies up to the window to take my place and make sure Angela is OK. I am concerned that my actions are causing Angela mental torment, and that is not very nice of me, even though it is unintentional. If I'd not been so tidy, I would have discarded the doorstop on the floor or in the bin and Angela might not have been so concerned. My mistake was to line up the doorstop exactly with her keyboard and the edge of the desk, so it was noticeable. I do have to understand things better and realise that my actions can have consequences I don't foresee. On the other paw, if I'd spent too long pondering the effects of my actions, I might have been caught in the act and banned from the library sine die, as they said in Ancient Rome.

"Are you alright, young Freddie?" asks Ron as I arrive back in the garden.

"I'm fine, thank you for asking, Ron," I say. "I hope that the blue-haired librarian is going to be alright, because I left the doorstop on her desk neatly and she noticed and was a little peeved and argued with her fellow staff members. I'm worried I have been sowing discord whereas I should provide peaceful feelings to people and my fellow animals, but especially humans who seem to get upset easily."

"Well, Freddie," says Rob, "you can't worry too much

about how your actions will affect other people, otherwise you'd end up doing nothing with your life for fear of upsetting something or someone else. You have to be true to yourself after all, be considerate and kind and unselfish whilst at the same time being true to what you want yourself to be."

"Have you read many books, Rob, because you should write a book as you're a natural philosopher?"

"All I've learned is from dealing with squirrels, dogs, and seagulls in the park. Books don't fit into our lifestyle well though I would like to read Plato, Nietzsche, and Marx. Not so much Wittgenstein, Heidegger, and Sartre. From what I've heard they're difficult to grasp."

"I wouldn't know," I say, "I've read none of their work, but from the few comments I've seen there's not a great deal of humour involved."

"That's correct, Freddie," says Rob, "that would probably make their work too dry for me. Oh, here's Jacqueline."

Jacqueline lands a few feet away and then hops over to where Rob and I are conversing.

"Hello, Freddie, you shouldn't worry about Angela, she's going to be fine, she was laughing with the other girl, Penny, just now. I think they're going to call in the vicar again, as they're not convinced the ghost has completely gone, so they will request another exorcism."

"A ghost with teeth?" I say. "That's an interesting idea, I hope I don't meet that ghost on my travels."

"Give the library a miss tomorrow," says Jacqueline, "I think they're on the lookout for unusual visitors such as guide dogs taking their owners to the toilet."

I giggle. "They do have vivid imaginations; I would have never thought of that. But if I do that again, but not tomorrow," I smile at Jacqueline as I say this, "I will have to remember to use more of my gums and less of my teeth, because the teeth marks were a clue."

"I'd make the most of your opportunities, Freddie," says Jacqueline, "because I think they're bound to realise eventually that the window is how you're gaining entry and close it, although it will be a last resort as Angela is a fresh-air fiend."

"Yes, you're right, they will, and I expect one day my humans will close the kitchen window and I won't be able to get out of the house, so I will have to find feasible alternatives. In fact, while I think of it, I will do it now. I will scamper around the library and the outside of the house and see whether there are any openings. There's no time like the present."

"I will come with you, Freddie," says Jacqueline. "I have seen a couple of open windows you might get through in the library. They usually keep the window open in the men's toilets because it smells so much, and I believe the door has one of those silver disks that opens the door when you touch it."

"Sounds wonderful," I say. "Are you coming, Rob?"

"No, I will fly up to our lookout point and give you 6 caws if I see anything for you to worry about."

"Right, that sounds like a plan," I say. "Let's explore."

I trot off towards the library, carefully avoiding the few humans who are walking in the opposite direction. I decide to go clockwise around the building. The north side is mainly glass panels allowing light in without dazzling the people inside on sunny days, a clever idea by the architects. The eastern side has the entrance plus meeting rooms and offices. Hugging the wall, I sidle towards the entrance and peer in through the glass by the sliding doors. I spot a couple of places where I would be out of sight to the librarians and most of the readers. If I lurk there, I can see outside and expect the doors to open when a heavy human activates the pressure pads in the floor. That is Plan B for escaping via the entrance. Plan A is jumping onto the pressure pads myself from a great height.

I continue around the outside and look in through a window. I see young people reading books around a table with picture cards placed on it. These look like items for children learning the alphabet and there's even a card C for Cat although the cat on this card is grey and has yellow eyes. This seems like stereotyping to me. Some of the children point at me and so I leave the ledge and turn right. They made this side of the building from sturdy dark bricks. I see Jacqueline perched on a window ledge.

"This is the window, Freddie," she says, "it's quite secluded here, and the window is usually open like this. Can you jump up?"

"I will try," I say, trying to measure the distance. I stand on my back paws and estimate it is five feet to the ledge, which is level and not sloping towards me. After a few deep breaths, I jump up. I get my front paws on the ledge and then pull myself up. I need to practice leaping as I feel weak.

Although I am on the ledge, there is still some work to do. I stand on my back paws again and extend my front paws until I can grip the frame of the open window. This is a bit like climbing the metal staircase on the side of the house. I can pull myself up slowly but surely until I can peer into the toilets. There are two strange drinking bowls by the wall and pieces of white paper lie around the white-tiled floor. It is a dazzling room and designed to make people keep their visit as short as possible.

"Do you see the silver disk on the wall, Freddie?" asks Jacqueline.

"I do," I say squinting, "I could jump up and hit that without a problem. Do you know if there's a similar disk on the other side of the door?"

"I don't, Freddie, I would imagine so, because they have to cater for disabled people on both sides of the door."

"That is very true," I reply. "I like your logic, Jacqueline. People don't suddenly become disabled in the toilet, do they?"

"I wouldn't have thought so," replies Jacqueline. "Anyway, do you think you could jump up to the window ledge inside?"

"It's the same height as this one, so I suppose I could do it and it is level, so I wouldn't slip off. That looks like an escape route or even an entry point if the librarian closes her window. Are there any other windows along here? Where's the ladies' toilet?"

"The Ladies is next to the Men's but without an exterior wall or window, Freddie, I heard one female explaining that to another a few weeks ago."

"Well listened, Jacqueline, anyway I think we should investigate further."

With that, I jump down onto the grass and stare up at the window. I am wondering whether I can improve my strength by finding somewhere similar to practice at home. The counters in the kitchen are too low, but I then think of the fridge. I can practice jumping from the kitchen floor onto the top of the fridge. The fridge is higher than the window ledge, but that would be OK. If I can jump onto the fridge top, then the window ledge won't be as difficult. I smile. It is always good to come up with a solution to a problem. I will have to build up to jumping onto the top of the fridge of course, firstly jumping onto the counter to refine my technique and to make sure I have the strength in my back legs, before trying the fridge with its smooth white sides and hard, rectangular surfaces.

"Come on, Freddie, you're day-dreaming," says Jacqueline as she hops down the path ahead of me.

"Right, just thinking about practising." I trot after Jacqueline, trying not to put my paws on the cracks in the paving, which brings bad luck.

"Planning is good," says Jacqueline. "There's another open window further down here, and I think it's a storeroom for stationery supplies."

"That sounds interesting...by the way, why do you hop along rather than fly?"

"Basically, it uses up less energy. Flying is overrated. We spend most of our time perched in trees arguing or walking around looking for insects."

"I think if I had wings, I'd fly everywhere," I say, looking up at the window and flapping my imaginary wings.

Jacqueline lands on the window ledge and peers inside. She turns, beckoning with her wing, and whispers, "There's someone in the room, jump up and see." I balance on my back paws and measure the distance carefully before leaping for the ledge. I do better this time and scramble onto the painted wood with less effort than before.

Inside, a small man wearing jeans and a green jumper is looking through the various cupboards and placing items such as pens, pencils, and printer paper into his bag. He hums to himself as he hurries through the room. Finally, he grabs two further items – an eraser and a small box of paper clips – and places them in a side pocket. Whistling, he glances up at the window and frowns as he sees two shapes through the glass. This sighting prompts him to leave the room.

"He's a thief," I say, "he's stealing other people's property."

"Yes, I'll see if he comes out of the entrance and then alert the others. We'll dive-bomb him and see if we can't get him to drop his bag. Those items are for everyone, not just him." With that Jacqueline flies off, cawing at her fellow crows.

I jump down from the window ledge and skedaddle round the side of the library to the entrance. There are 6 crows lined-up on the telephone wires. All of them are facing the sliding doors. I jump into a small tree and lurk. The crows caw, and I see the man, who is now wearing a leather jacket over his jumper, walking out.

As soon as he emerges, the crows fly close to his head,

cawing loudly and creating a scene. The man puts up his hands to protect himself. The librarians inside the building come to the glass to find out what the commotion is. As the bag is on the ground, I take my chance. I run over to the bag. The side pocket is open. I spy the box of paper clips, grab it with my teeth, and run over to where the librarians are watching and place the box on the ground in full view. Then I do the same with the eraser. The crows are squawking loudly and pecking at the man's hands, which are clasped over his head. I retire to the tree to lurk again.

The lady from the front desk comes outside and picks up the paper clips and the eraser. She walks over to where the man is flapping his hands at the crows, who retire to the wires overhead, their work done.

"Where did these stationery items come from, Danny?"

"I do not know, Sheila," replies the man, staring at the crows who glare back at him.

"A cat pulled them out of your bag and deposited them in front of the entrance."

"A cat? What cat?"

"It scampered off as cats do, but it knew exactly where to go, so do you mind if I inspect your bag, Danny, and see what I find?"

"Sheila, I can explain..." says Danny, his voice trailing off.

"We'll examine your bag inside, if that's OK, out of the view of the local wildlife?" says Sheila pointing up at the crows.

"I'm not sure what I did to upset them," replies Danny before picking up the bag and heading inside.

I miaow with delight at the apparent apprehension of the thief named Danny. Overhead the crows seem to be celebrating as they are cawing and bouncing up and down on the wires. I laugh at them. They spot me and fly down into the tree.

"Well done, Freddie," says Reg, "you certainly exposed him as a thief."

"I couldn't have done it without you," I reply, "as you were distracting him, he completely ignored me."

"It was a great idea to pick up those items and deposit them in front of the librarians," says Ron.

"Well, you should make it obvious sometimes," I reply. "You should create an image that will stick in their mind, an image that is out of the ordinary, unusual, and memorable. I think a cat running along with a small box of paper clips in his mouth fits the bill."

"That's true, Freddie," says Rob, "very true, I will certainly never forget it myself."

"Well, that's good. I'm glad we've done something together, we've achieved something, and I hope that the Danny person now feels he did wrong."

"He seemed to be in a state of denial to me," says Rob, "as though he was going to blame someone else for his thieving ways."

"You have to own up and take responsibility," I say, "like when I vomit, I can't really deny it's happened, can I?"

"I suppose not," says Jacqueline.

"It's there in front of me," I continue, "so you just have to be honest."

The crows nod in agreement, as there isn't much they can say about the truth of this statement. Vomit speaks for itself.

"Anyway, I should look around the outside of the house now, as I need to find a new method of exit and entrance, in case the kitchen window is closed by the humans."

"We've had a look around for you," says Reg, "and we've not seen anything open downstairs and only the kitchen window and toilet window open upstairs. The toilet window just leads to brickwork and a downspout from the roof, so you could slide down that, but I'm not sure you could climb up it."

"The spout has rings around it, every two feet, which are set into the bricks to bring solidity to the structure," says Ron, "you might pull yourself up from one ring to the next, gripping the rings with you claws, back and front, but it would be tiring especially the first few times."

"I'd like to try it now and find out how much fitter I have to be," I reply. "I know I have to jump onto the top of the fridge from the kitchen floor, but that's inside exercise, I have to do some outside exercise too."

I scamper around the fence and jump over the garden gate with ease, as I feel energised after talking about my future strength tests with the crows. I stop and look up the white spout to the bathroom window and it appears to be halfway to the grey sky. Standing on my back paws, I reach for the first ring. It is flush with the spout, and I can't grip it.

"Try the back, Freddie, the spout is about 5 inches away from the wall, so you could pull yourself up, like you do on the trellis," suggests Reg.

"Good idea," I say. "Oh yes, it's easier here, thanks, Reg."

I grip the ring and drag myself. The problem is having all four paws in the same place on the ring. Eventually, I sort them out and reach for the next ring. I get to the fourth ring but am exhausted by this time. I put my front paws around the spout and slide downwards gently, being careful not to catch my fur on any of the rings.

I reach the bottom of the spout and am surprised to see Rufus waiting amongst the crows.

"You looked as though you were getting the hang of the technique," says Jacqueline.

"That's the important thing," says Reg, "it's the technique that's the most important, the wrong technique will sap your strength. Isn't that right, Rufus?"

Rufus nods. "Most assuredly, Reg, and I think you might benefit from learning to climb a tree, young Freddie, it's the coordination of left and right you should work on. You will have to climb down tail first, almost like you'll be in reverse, but it will be better with your claws as they will only be effective with your head facing upwards."

"I think you're right, Rufus," I reply. "My claws are for grasping things towards me, rather than for weight bearing away from me. When can we go climbing?"

"I will be back from the park at noon tomorrow," says Rufus, "so if you meet me at the bottom of my tree at noon, then we should be able to climb the tree."

"Sounds great, Rufus, and to return the favour I will take you to the library, though not tomorrow as they're having thief problems, so everyone will be slightly nervous and keeping their eyes peeled for strange happenings."

"Humans have thief problems, too?" asks Rufus. "What were they stealing? Books?"

"Paper clips, paper, pencils, pens, and an eraser," says Jacqueline.

"None of those are edible," says Rufus. "Why would anyone steal those things?"

"Greed," says Rob, "I think he was going to sell those things for personal gain."

"That's terrible," says Rufus. "Human beings are very selfish sometimes, just thinking of themselves. What will happen to the thief?"

"He was going to be relieved of his duties," says Ron, "I heard him being shouted at by the Chief Librarian. And from what Danny admitted, this wasn't the first time it has happened."

"He's only got away with it in the past because we weren't looking at him through the window, when he was stealing things," says Jacqueline.

"Could you use that window to gain access to the library?" asks Ron.

"Only partially," I say. "The room appears locked and there isn't a silver disk on the wall, so I couldn't use the window really to get in and out, other than perhaps to hide in."

"There's only one option, other than the blue-haired librarian's window, and that's the men's toilets," says Jacqueline.

"It's an alternative," I say, "and I might use it the next time I try to gain entry to the library."

Five caws ring out from the tallest tree in the area.

"One of your humans is coming," says Reg.

"It will be the male human, walking from the train," I say, "so I should wish you all a very pleasant evening and I will see you tomorrow."

With that I scuttle around the house and climb up the thin metal staircase, wishing the rose a pleasant evening on the way, before squeezing in through the window. I am back in the kitchen. I size up the fridge and think I'll try it. I jump up and get my paws onto the top, but don't have the strength to pull myself up, so I slide down the front of the white appliance before landing on my back paws. I resolve to try again, but now it's time to sleep or appear to sleep under the couch. I close my eyes just before John walks in – I can hear his socks sliding across the wood, having taken his shoes off outside.

Chapter 9

Today

I WAKE UP TO FIND sunshine pouring through the Venetian blinds onto the wooden floor. I slept really well, perhaps not surprising given all the climbing I'd done the previous today in the name of adventure. At breakfast, I am respectful towards the kibbles and the cat food placed in my bowl. I know it is going to be a good day when Gemma smiles at me and wishes me 'Good morning' without a sneer. I return the smile before heading back upstairs to read *The Third Man* by Graham Greene, which I'd started the previous evening after the humans had gone to bed and after I'd been unable to find *Brighton Rock*. Apparently, Graham never intended for *The Third Man* to be read by the likes of me. He wrote the book as practice for the screenplay of the film but being famous Graham's publishers produced it anyway and I am very thankful.

I must try to find a travel book of Vienna when I next go to the library, in the European travel section. The Ferris Wheel and the sewers sound amazing, but I'm not sure whether there will be any pictures of the sewers as they will be dark and so wouldn't make wonderful photos. Often, I wonder how I would travel to a foreign city? Would the airline allow me on the plane? Would I purchase a ticket, or would they employ me as a rodent eliminator and so I would not have to pay? The problem is, I don't own any human money, but Gemma tells me I could use the humans' credit card to pay, but that would be dishonest and besides, I'm still not sure how I would get through customs and onto the plane. I recall they write guidebooks for humans and not for cats, so information about circumventing customs and sneaking onto the plane won't be available. But at least I won't need to check in any baggage, as I only possess one set of clothes. All cats speak the same language, at least that's my understanding, so I won't need a phrasebook.

Anyway, I've distracted myself from the book, so I read again, keeping a careful note of the time, as I must meet Rufus at noon. I will give myself 20 minutes to chat to the crows on my way to Rufus's tree. Suddenly, sirens blare and seem to get closer to the house. The crows start to caw. I glance out of the front window where two or three people are grappling with each other, trying to gain control of what looks like a large piece of wood. The police then arrive and point revolvers at the three people involved in the fracas. Each puts their hands in the air and the piece of wood falls to the ground, where it's quickly snatched away by an officer.

I make a careful note of where I am in *The Third Man*; the humans don't own a surfeit of bookmarks, and then use the litter tray before squeezing through the kitchen window out into the garden. The crows aren't around, so I pad over to the garden gate and jump up to where I can observe what is happening. There are flashing lights all around. The police have handcuffed the three protagonists. Rob flutters down and lands next to me.

"What's happened?" I ask. "What were those three people doing?"

"Well, Freddie," replies Rob, "one of the three is Danny, the thief. He brought his rifle to the library and was trying to shoot us crows, whom he held responsible for him being caught red-handed. Thankfully, we saw him coming and kept out of sight, but as he was pointing his gun in the air, one librarian came outside and asked him what he was doing. Danny then pointed the gun at him, which was when the skirmish really started because two passers-by tried to grab the rifle from Danny, and he wouldn't let go of it."

"It's a good thing you always post a sentinel crow, a watching crow who sees people coming and can warn everyone."

"Yes, that's why we do it. Danny was also shouting about the cat that shopped him, I will tell you that."

"He must mean me," I say, "but that's OK, because he doesn't know where I live. Presumably the police will charge with him with a public-order offence?"

"Well," says Rob, "plus carrying an offensive weapon, threatening to use the offensive weapon, and endangering life."

"Why would he do that?"

"He is still upset about losing his job from yesterday and people must always blame someone else, point the finger at someone else, in his case point the gun at someone else, rather than admitting he did something wrong by stealing those few small items."

"Yes," I say, "as usual you're right about philosophical matters, Rob. I am sorry about him losing his job. He could just give those things back, couldn't he?"

"Well, you shouldn't feel guilty, young Freddie, you shouldn't feel guilty as you did the right thing, dishonesty should never have its reward, and he had stolen items before from the library, he admitted that himself, so he's only got himself to blame. One day he'll realise he did something wrong and perhaps he'll repent or forgive himself."

"We won't be around then, I would imagine, because he'll be in prison for a few years with all those charges against him."

"I hope you are right, Freddie, I hope you're right. Sometimes the courts can be lenient, but if his rifle isn't licensed, then he could be in big trouble."

"Oh, I understand," I say, "I didn't know they had to be licensed, I suppose it's a bit like James Bond, 007, a license to kill. I wonder if Danny has a number like that, perhaps he's 008."

"James Bond was a fictional spy, but perhaps all the licenses begin with 00?"

"What's going on, folks?" asks Rufus. He jumps on the gate and is holding a nut between his front paws.

Rob gives Rufus a brief explanation of what has happened.

"That's terrible," comments Rufus. "He shouldn't be allowed to wield a gun and try to shoot at any living creature." He chews at the nut.

The police place each of the three people in separate

vehicles, pressing their heads down so they don't receive a blow to their cranium, which is kind of the police. The blue lights flash as the little convoy heads towards the main road and the big city in the distance.

Five caws replace the sirens.

"Well, well," says Rob, "look what's here. A man with a small dog and even smaller video, pointing at us."

I stare at the man, and it isn't the Walt man of 'Penny and Walt' fame, which is a relief.

"Is he a wildlife photographer?" says Rufus, reversing his posture and shaking his tail at him. This inspires me to do the same as did Rob.

"This is a different view," I say. "I can tell, Rufus, you would almost certainly love to sit on the machine at the library and create a work of art with me. Imagine how that would appear if we included Holly."

"It would amaze," says Rufus, "but the only thing is, I understand you have to sign works of art in order for them to be genuinely worth something."

"You do, Rufus," replies Rob, "you do, but these works of art normally only become valuable many years after the artist has passed away and even if you were still alive, the value would be in human currency not in nuts."

"He could buy some nuts with the currency," I suggest, trying to be helpful.

Rufus laughs and says, "I might want to try something other than nuts, because I only eat nuts as there's not much else to eat around here for me, I might like to try Croque Monsieur or toast or muesli."

"Muesli is the same oats that horses eat," I say, "but toast would be good, it's quite crunchy and is basically lightly burned bread, and I love bread, but I find it constipates me a little."

"Crows don't have that problem with anything," says Rob, "but I digress, I should leave you two to your tree climbing exploits as we have a weekly meeting on your house roof, Freddie, about our findings of the past 7 days."

"Thanks, Rob," I say as Rob flies off. "OK, Rufus, let's go climbing and discover what happens. I'm hoping that my climbing attempts yesterday don't have any lasting effects on my muscles, though I don't seem sore."

"You are a strong young cat, Mr. Freddie, so you will be fine. By the way, that man is still watching us, and I would expect he will probably film you as you climb up the tree."

"That's fine, as long as he doesn't film me coming down the tree, which is what most concerns me."

"You'll be fine, Freddie, let's climb the tree, my tree, and build your confidence, which is the principal thing I suspect."

I laugh and follow Rufus as he jumps across the grass towards the base of the tree.

"Here we are," he says, "base camp. Now humour me here, try to climb the tree and let me watch you."

I nod and put my front paws on the bark. I pull myself up for a few feet but can't help noticing that my paws are getting further apart, and my nose and belly are almost rubbing on the trunk of the tree. If I carry on much further, I will be stuck and have to apply reverse. Or drop off, which I don't want captured on film, a cat parachuting without a parachute. I could visualise the title now, however it might make the cat memes that people like John watch on social media, so I might become famous.

"OK, Freddie, please put yourself into reverse and come down the tree," says Rufus. "I have seen enough, and you need to change your technique."

"OK, Rufus," I say, gingerly stretching my back paws down the tree about 10 inches at a time and making sure I hook them into the bark before resting my weight on them. Every time I attach my claws to the tree, I whisper my apologies to the tree, as their sharpness might hurt the tree and this brings me sadness. After about 5 minutes, I am back down with my squirrel friend.

"The first thing you have to do is gain more confidence descending otherwise it will take you about an hour to come down my tree," says Rufus, shaking his head slightly, "so climb up one cat length and stay there."

I climb up one cat's length.

"Right, Freddie, you're moving both back paws at once and then holding on like grim death with both your front paws, as though you're dangling from the trunk. My suggestion is to coordinate left and right, move your back right and front right together and then move your two left paws together. Try that from where you are."

I try Rufus's suggestion and it seems strange at first, but eventually I get the hang of it. Each time I reverse, I am more confident, and after about ten goes, I have my reversing well synchronised.

"That looks a lot better," says Rufus. "Now when you go

upwards, do the same synchronised movements, left and right, but stretch your paws in a straight line, not out to the side, that way you will stay the same distance from the tree all the way up and not find your nose rubbing against the bark, like you are doing now."

"Thank you, Rufus. It seems so obvious when you say it," I say, starting my way up the tree. "Oh, this is easier, now I'll come back down." I am getting used to the technique and movements required quickly.

"Try halfway to the top," says Rufus, "that's approximately where the first major branch is on the right as you're heading upwards."

I climb steadily to the branch and reverse down at about the same speed. I do this twice and am pleased with my efforts.

"How did that seem?" asks Rufus.

"Well, it feels as though I'm using muscles in places where I didn't know I had any muscles," I say, stretching my back paws to ease some of the tension.

I spy the man filming us with his small camera.

"Has he been there all the time?" I ask.

"I'm not sure, Freddie, it really doesn't bother me, he might have been, but all he will have seen of me is my tail and he's welcome to that."

"He's been filming me climbing up the tree, hoping I would fall off. That's not very nice, is it? I will climb up again, this time with my tail in the air, just so he can view my disapproval of his unwanted intrusion into my newest hobby."

I duly climb up the tree, wiggling my hips a little as I go. Even a Buddhist cat should have some privacy when he's enjoying his leisure time and learning a new skill. Holding my tail up straight adds another item for me to concentrate on, particularly as I apologise to the tree each time I dig my claws into its bark.

When I reach the branch, Rufus scampers up beside me.

"I've had an idea," he says, "even though it's a waste of good food, it will be worth it." Rufus forages in a crack in the tree and pulls out two nuts. He looks at where the man is and runs along a branch, so he's above his head. He drops a nut.

"Heh, heh, stop that," the man shouts, "you're a bad squirrel and you're a terrible cat. Don't throw things at me."

I manoeuvre onto the branch, so I am out of sight from below.

Rufus drops the nut and hits the man's shoulder. Rufus runs to me.

The man shouts again.

One of the community police, who'd attended the earlier incident, comes over to him.

"Is there a reason you're shouting at the tree, sir?" she asks.

"Yes, a squirrel and a cat are throwing nuts at me."

"A cat is throwing nuts at you from a tree?"

"Yes, they're in it together."

"Are they? Why would they do that?"

"I'm a keen videographer and I was filming the cat climbing the tree, I'll show you if you like?"

"That won't be necessary, sir. Cats don't throw things, they're creatures that are not really designed for throwing items at passers-by. Scratching is more their style."

"It's up with the squirrel." The man points upwards.

"Walk away, sir, walk away and shout at another tree further away, perhaps the oak tree down there? We're still taking statements here, because of the earlier incident, and it's an unwelcome distraction to have someone shouting into a tree while we're doing our routine work."

"You don't believe me; you reckon I'm a nutter."

The officer gestures towards the oak tree, "That tree will be far enough away. Perhaps the squirrel and cat will be along later to pelt you with acorns? I tell you what, if they do that, come and tell us when we've finished our work and we'll arrest them."

The man turns on his heel and walks away.

"Serves him right," I say, "that's karma at work I tell you. Karma is present at all times in all places, he should have been respectful towards us, and he chose not to be, and the universe caused a correction to occur."

"Did it?" says Rufus.

"It did, yes. You're sceptical about my assertion?"

"All that bothers me is that I've wasted two good nuts on that man."

"You can climb down and get them."

"Well, no, the nuts hit him. Humans wash their clothes and hair with funny stuff that leaves a discernible smell on my nuts and makes them taste peculiar. Shampoo and washer liquid they're called."

"Yes, shampoo, not real poo," I say, giggling. I'd seen a picture in a book of a smiling Buddha, so I know it is OK to make jokes occasionally and still be a Buddhist.

"Should we find you some more nuts?" I say.

"Yes, but let's go the opposite way to the man," says Rufus. "Climb down the other side of the tree, so the police don't observe you, and we'll head to the oak tree in the other direction. I'll go via the branches and telephone wires, and we'll meet there. We shouldn't be seen together until the trouble has blown over," says Rufus, winking conspiratorially before heading upwards towards another branch.

I climb down the other side of the tree, making sure no one is watching me or filming me, before scooting away towards the rendezvous at the oak tree. The time in the oak tree is productive and yields several acorns for Rufus to enthuse about. I practise my tree climbing technique in a different tree as he scampers back to his home tree with his finds. We are like two old friends who have known each other for years and don't need to say much. It's strange how that happens with some friends and not others. It could also be because Rufus is always eating something and has his mouth full at all times. Eventually, Rufus finds enough acorns and calls it a day.

"Freddie, did you want to try going back through the trees? There's a safe route along sturdy branches you should be able to follow."

"How sturdy is sturdy? I weigh more than you. And there's no telephone lines to crawl along?"

"No telephone lines and branches that will take your weight. There's not much jumping either, perhaps one foot but no more."

"OK, Rufus, I will try my best. Go first but don't go too far ahead as you know the route and I don't."

"I will go first and wait for you, don't worry, I will point out where to land."

"Thank you, Rufus. OK, let's try this – after you."

Rufus bounds away, and I watch carefully before following him, noting where he lands. It turns out to be a straightforward route and I thank the trees for their kindness in growing so close, allowing a footpath for animals in the sky above the humans.

We arrive at Rufus's tree and arrange to go over to the park later in the week to visit the garden crows, who are taking their turn on the other side of the road.

With that, I nonchalantly climb down the tree and head back to the house. I am tired after the exercise and my shoulder and hip muscles are sore. I fall asleep under the sofa and the rest of the day passes peacefully.

Chapter 10

Today

I WAKE UP THIS MORNING – I know I should compose lyrics for Blues songs, which often start with these words. What Blues songs rarely mention is that out of the window I see Holly the Hamster running in a northerly direction, towards the park. This can only mean one thing; I am visiting the library again and with an accomplice this time. I will have to practice patience today as Holly will rely on me and yet she wants to know what books are available. I will also have to appear mellow, so as not to raise suspicion about my activities later in the day.

The man who videoed my climbing yesterday will presumably show his film to anyone and everyone who he can bore to death with it. Eventually, he will knock on my house door and tell the humans about their cat and its climbing exploits, or a neighbour will tell them. I think about this as I poo and as I eat my kibbles individually. I doubt John and Mary will bother. They won't worry that I could get in and out of the house – what would concern them is that I didn't hurt myself when I was outside or got myself stuck somewhere I couldn't escape from and they wouldn't be able to help me. I know they love me, and I love them back. I'm like their child and they want me to have a good life, free from worry and hurt, so if I show them I'm fit and healthy and happy then they'll know everything is well with me.

After breakfast, I practise jumping onto the top of the fridge and manage to scramble onto the top each time, but what I want is a nice, clean leap onto the top without touching the sides. This is my aim.

"You like it up there, don't you, Mr. Freddie cat?" says John, stroking me under the chin before he leaves for work.

I miaow and purr a little. He doesn't take me off the fridge, a good sign, as it doesn't irritate him to see me there. I can carry on leaping. After Mary leaves I have a morning snooze and then I slip through the window, climb down the metal staircase in double-quick time, give the Lancashire rose some encouragement in her quest for the top, and head towards the window of Holly the Hamster who is walking in her wheel.

"Hello, Holly," I say, "I remembered."

"I knew you would," she replies. "So, they have left my cage unlocked and the window is open so I should be able to come out onto the ledge where you are."

"Sounds good. I will make some room for you. Are you going to ride on my back?"

"I would like that," replies Holly. "I get far too much exercise daily as it is, so someone else carrying me is a wonderful idea."

"I'm running a feline taxi service," I say, "but I don't mind as I would like some company at the library."

Holly pushes open the door of her cage and climbs through the open window, before jumping on to the ledge.

"Can you get down onto the fence from here?" I ask.

"I'll have to hold on to you," says Holly. "I'll put my paws around your neck and hopefully you'll land softly."

"Don't worry," I reply, "I always land softly and the climb up to the library window isn't steep, so you will be fine."

Holly climbs up my back and grips the fur at the side of my neck. I flop off the ledge and land on the fence and then run along the top until I come to the place where the fence is only two feet high, and I drop onto the grass.

"What's it like?" I ask.

"It's wonderful, I'm a pillion passenger on a cat and it's such a wonderful change to have someone else do all the work."

Reg, Rob, Ron, and Jacqueline land close to us.

"Morning, Freddie, are you hamster napping Holly?" asks Ron.

"I've never heard that word before," I giggle, "but I am taking Holly for a trip to the library. I'm giving her a lift, so she can have a day off from running in her wheel."

"It's fun," says Holly, "I've never been inside a library before, so I'm hoping to learn something today."

"Well, there's been some excitement at the library recently," says Reg, "as Freddie will tell you, so just be careful both of you, that no one sees you around, because all the humans will have a heightened state of awareness."

"I know my way around a little better now." I hope I sound reassuring.

Jacqueline nods. "Freddie has three escape routes now, not that he'll need them I'm sure, but it's good to have a Plan B and a sound Plan C."

"Any more than three would be confusing," says Rob, "I think three plans is enough for anyone."

"I agree," says Holly. "Normally, I've got one plan, which is to survive until the end of the day."

Everyone has a pleasant laugh about this comment.

"Right, I think we should go," I say. "Is the librarian's window open? She'll be going for lunch soon, so we have to take our chance to at least get into the library."

"The librarian's window is open and the last time I looked, the lid was up on the photocopier," says Rob. "It's her blind spot, she uses the machine a lot on some days and leaves the lid open for convenience. Humans can be lazy like that sometimes."

"I'm amazed you know so much. Where do you get your information from?" asks Holly.

"We talk amongst ourselves, and we notice a lot of what's happening around us, so we know many things," says Jacqueline.

"We should go, Holly, don't forget to hold on to my fur," I say, "and I promise not to run under any low branches. I will meet you all later after we've had our adventure in the library."

"How long are you planning to be inside?" asks Ron.

"About 2 hours," I reply.

"We'll keep an eye open for you," says Reg, "just in case you run into any problems inside."

"Thank you," I say, "it's great to have such wonderful friends."

With that, I trot off towards the vine. Holly giggles.

"Are you OK, Holly?" I ask.

"Yes, it's wonderful to relax for once and let the world go by, although I think the human we ran by was startled by us."

"We can't go around conforming to what other people expect, Holly, because we'd never be true to ourselves then, would we?"

"You're correct, Freddie, unless you were in a rut and didn't realise it."

"True, Holly, but who recognises they're in a rut? You normally have to have it pointed out to you by someone else. Anyway, here's the vine. Keep your head down and grip my fur, as I climb. It's a gentle gradient, so we should be OK."

"I'm ready," squeaks Holly as she stares up at the window, the first destination of this adventure.

I smile as I ascend the vine towards the opening into the blue-haired librarian's world. I hope Holly the Hamster has a head for heights, otherwise we might be in trouble. I can feel her gripping my fur, but not too tightly, as we approach the window. I arrive at the ledge and allow Holly to slide off onto the white surface.

"How are you feeling, Holly?" I ask.

"Shaky," she replies, "but the air is certainly fresh up here."

"It is. This is like our Everest base camp," I say, "you should take some breaths and get used to the altitude. Could you climb down that vine, do you reckon?"

"I probably could, though not too quickly. I suppose you're thinking ahead in case we get split up for any reason?"

"Yes, I suppose I am, although I doubt that will happen. Now, where was it you want to go?"

"I want to have a go on the photocopier," says Holly, "and then visit the Travel section, so I can look at the pictures of The Pyramids in Egypt. I also want to visit the Pets section, so I can find out what hamsters are supposed to eat."

"Right, sounds exciting. I know the ancient Egyptians adored cats, so that should be an interesting read. I'll peer through the window and find out if the coast is clear."

I take a sneaky look around the side of the window and am pleased there's an empty office with the photocopier lid in the air. Holly and I can make some art together.

"OK, Holly, we can go. I think the plan will be for us to exit the building via the men's toilets on the ground floor. I've not left that way before, so it will be a brilliant experiment. First, let's make some art."

We jump onto a box of paper and then on to the glass surface.

"It's warm isn't it?" says Holly. "I could sleep on this although it is bright."

"Yes, it would be nice to sleep on," I say. "What kind of art should we make?"

"With the tails at right angles and then opposite," says Holly. "I've been thinking about this, and I reckon that would be quite artistic."

"Let's do that, but not too much, as I don't want the librarian to have a mental breakdown and think there's another ghost in here. She's an agreeable person and doesn't deserve to feel persecuted."

"I understand," replies Holly. "Can I press the button you told me about? I can be the artist then and you've done it before."

I smile, "Of course, we'll have to move around as the button is here." I gesture with my paw to the red square. I check the print on both sides option is selected.

We inch our way around each other and then sit at right angles with our tails touching. Holly presses the button, and the machine makes its internal gestating noises before birthing the artwork.

"Where's the art?" asks Holly.

"It's here," I say, "and I have to say...it looks odd."

Holly stares down at the paper.

"Is that really my backside?" she asks. "It's upsetting. I thought it would be lovelier…"

"It's set to black and white," I reply, "so it's an overdramatic simplification of your true self, isn't it, it's not an accurate representation of the essential you."

"There's an absence of colour, that's true. Oh well, I didn't think art would be like that, so self-revealing, I'm not sure I like it, can we recycle it or put it in the bin?"

"Well, if you really dislike it, then we can try to put it in the bin."

I reach down and paw the art onto the floor. Holly jumps down via a box and picks up the paper in her teeth. I scamper over to the bin, stretch, and place my paws on the rim before pulling it over gradually towards me. When it hits the floor,

Holly runs into it until she reaches the bottom. The paper is inside the bin.

"Can we put the bin upright?" I ask. "It looks messy like that, and she'll notice if it's on its side."

"How?" says Holly, peeling a sweet wrapper from her paw.

"Can you burrow under it with your nose and then I can put my paw under it and lift it up? We should put the bin closer to the desk, so it won't fall over the other way."

"I might hurt my nose if I try to burrow under it."

"OK, I will try to put my paw under the edge."

I stand by the bin and try to lift it up with my right paw. I raise it a little and Holly puts her nose under it and tries to burrow. She wiggles her hips, and the bin rises a little before falling back.

"I'm trapped," she says, "I'm stuck, I'm stuck, please put your paw in and release the pressure."

I put my front leg in further and raise the bin, but I don't have the strength to lift it upwards and sideways. Holly can reverse out, which is a relief.

"We'll have to leave it like that," she says, "we're wasting valuable reading time."

"I agree, let's go, but first we should check the corridor and make sure no one is coming. We'll go to the Pets section first and then head down the backstairs to the Travel section. They're almost under each other."

"Sounds like a plan. I'll find out, I'm smaller than you," says Holly, and creeps up to the threshold of the door and looks both ways.

"It's clear," she says.

I scamper out and jump up to hit the silver disk on the wall. My legs are stronger than last time, as I jump too high and have to push the disk with my paws on the way down.

The door shudders open to reveal mostly empty tables with a few people reading the newspapers on the left-hand side of the floor.

"The Pets section is to the right," I say, "let's scuttle along the wall here and then turn left by the first bookcase."

"OK," says Holly, "I will follow you."

I run as fast as I can along the skirting board and veer left towards Pets. Holly is behind me all the way.

"Hamsters are down here," I say, "on the lowest shelf."

"I can only see guinea pig books," says Holly.

"The hamsters are here," I say padding along the rack and pulling at a slim volume. It falls into the gap between the rows of books. I turn it around with some nimble paw work in a confined space so Holly can flick through the book while I stand on the open pages.

"Did you find the right page?"

"Yes, I reckon so. I'm looking at the diet suggestions and it says the favourite foods of hamsters include, cooked beans, cucumbers, apples, broccoli, dog biscuits, carrots, and rice. Roborovskis, which are dwarf hamsters about 2 inches long, like Chinese cabbage, birdseed, and sweet corn. Syrian hamsters, which are also called Golden Hamsters, like a wide range of fruits, vegetables, and grains, basically anything they can get their teeth into."

"Which hamster are you?"

"I'm a Chinese hamster, my tail's long, which is one giveaway, so my owners give me vegetables and some chicken as a substitute for the insects I would normally eat in the deserts of northern China. It appears my handlers are giving me the right things, although the male gives me his broccoli and pretends he's eaten it himself, as I gobble everything up quickly."

"Don't they feed you regularly then?"

"They do, Freddie, I'm a glutton, a greedy guts if you like."

"Well, I'm a Buddhist cat. I eat slowly as I bow to each kibble and mouthful of food before I eat it out of respect and thank them for allowing me to eat them. I'm trying to be generous and kind."

"That's interesting, presumably you have no other hungry cat eating at the same time as you."

"Well, only Gemma, but she's not a greedy cat and never tries to eat my food. She thinks I'm odd to treat my food with respect, but I suppose at least she doesn't eat my food before I've finished."

"She is showing you some respect then, Freddie," says Holly.

"I suppose she is," I reply. "I'd never really thought of it like that." Then I ponder what I've just heard myself say while Holly continues to read about what a healthy hamster should eat in the modern age.

"Mmm, well, I think they're feeding me the correct food and in the right amounts. I'm going to the toilet the correct number of times too, which is good."

"Do they ever take you to the vet for a check-up?"

"No, what's a vet, an animal doctor?"

"Yes, that's what a vet is, they always give me a thorough examination, which I don't always appreciate, especially when they take my temperature."

"They don't put the thermometer in your mouth then?"

"No, they don't – it's rather uncomfortable to be honest, Holly, but it's not as much of a shock the second time as it is the first."

"Yes, you know what's coming and can brace yourself. Anyway, I think we can find Egypt now. I've seen all I want here. I feel reassured."

"That's good, we'll leave the book here, as I'm not sure we could put it back in its proper place. Let's see if the coast is clear. We have to run down the steps over there to the floor below and then go straight ahead when we go through the door."

"Right, I will follow you again."

"I will just check there's no one near us, as I don't want people to discover us, at least not just yet, because we have to find Egypt first."

I scout the surroundings. There are some people close by, looking at dog books. I gesture to Holly that we will have to wait for the people to leave. They are talking amongst themselves a lot about chihuahuas which are yappy dogs in my experience. Those people seem like ideal chihuahua owners to me. Immediately, I admonish myself because as a Buddhist cat I shouldn't be thinking things like this; I must keep my sense of mischief in check and not think unkind thoughts about other people, even if they deserve them. I should not judge other people like this and it's wrong of me to do it. If I'm not careful, I might reincarnate as a chihuahua or even worse a chihuahua owner. I close my eyes and meditate on my indiscretions and how I should behave in these situations.

Suddenly, there is a scream. I open my eyes. Angela appears clutching our artwork.

"It's time to leave, Holly. Egypt will have to wait until next time. Angela is providing a diversion and we should take advantage. Let's go down the backstairs to the men's toilets."

Holly nods and jumps onto my back, gripping my fur tightly. I glance around. The path is clear. I land softly on the floor and skedaddle down the stairs, heading down two floors before turning to my right. Behind me I hear a voice say,

"There's a cat being ridden by a small rat and they're going to the toilet."

I carry on.

"Holly, please climb off me for a second while I jump up to open the door," I say calmly.

"Of course," says Holly and jumps on to the floor.

I jump and hit the silver disk with my front paws. The door opens slowly, and we scuttle inside onto the white-tiled floor with some discarded brown paper towels lying around the metal bin. The path is clear now. We will jump onto the sink, and then onto the window ledge and vacate the premises.

"Holly, hold on tight."

She grabs my fur. I summon my energy and tilt backwards slightly as footsteps approach.

"The cat definitely went in here, perhaps it needed to go to the toilet."

I hurl myself upwards and land on the pure white sink. The door opens again. I leap onto the ledge, and we sneak through the gap to the outside. We both sit still and listen.

"Let's find them," says the security guard, keeping low to the ground. "There aren't too many places to hide. Let's keep the door closed so that they're trapped." The door closes. The security guard moves each of the pieces of paper with his foot while the man with him looks in the cubicle.

"There's nothing here," says the man in the cubicle, "but I'm sure they came in here, because the cat jumped up and hit the opening mechanism with its paws and there's nowhere else for them to go."

"Not unless they're in the bin," says the guard, "but wait, if the cat could jump up and open the door then he might jump out of the window. We should have a gander."

I motion to Holly to follow me through the bushes to the floor, where we make our way to the pavement. Jacqueline lands close to us.

"You should go the long way around," she says, "the humans are predictably taking the shortcut and will be here in 10 seconds. In a moment, we'll start our blitzkrieg impression, so you should skedaddle back to your house while that's happening."

"What's blitzkrieg?" asks Holly.

"It's basically dive-bombing, screeching, and unmercifully attacking the enemy," replies Jacqueline, "you'll find out in a few seconds."

Holly and I thank Jacqueline, run along the concrete, and hide under a rhododendron bush so we can view the window. Sure enough, the security guard and the other man appear at the corner slightly out-of-breath and look around in the undergrowth for evidence of animals that recently escaped from the library. The security guard inspects the window ledge and sees nothing too suspicious by his reaction. Suddenly black shapes surround the two men, harassing them unmercifully. The corvine Stukas are in action again.

We run off and reach the safety of the garden, where I give Holly a lift back to her home. We agree we should try this again the following week as the library staff would be more aware of suspicious activities for the rest of the week, but human nature being what it was they would soon lapse into their old routines by the beginning of the following week. I decide this is a good time to get some horizontal exercise, and I run around Holly's house fence without being attacked by gravity.

I saunter across to my garden, where the crows are waiting for me. "Thank you for your help," I say. "We escaped thanks to you."

"You're welcome, young Freddie," says Stan, "it was a good bit of exercise for us, that gets the blood flowing. Jacqueline is doing some eaves-dropping at the window to make sure the librarian is alright as it quite upset her to see two animal backsides on the same piece of paper – in her mind the ghost problem has become worse and not better."

"I hope she's alright," I say, "I don't like animals to suffer like that."

"Here comes Jacqueline," says Seb.

She lands close to us, and we wait for her to catch her breath.

"Well, they still think there's a ghost problem although they can't explain why one of their customers thought he saw a cat and a rat – that's their word not mine, apologies to Holly – running towards the toilet on the ground floor. However, the cat and the rat then disappeared, lending credence to the ghost idea, so they will call in the vicar again to perform another exorcism, so I'd steer clear of the library, Freddie, for the next 2 days while tensions remain high."

I nod and say I will definitely do that.

"Angela is upset but says she will get over it and she thought the two backsides were more artistic than one, that there was more balance to the image, but she will still shred it."

"A lot of great art has been destroyed," I say sadly, "but at least we can recreate that piece should the need arise at some future date."

"You should come over to the park tomorrow, Freddie," says Sid, "and leave the people at the library to their own devices for a few days."

"Yes, I think you're right. And it will be good to head over the road with Rufus and discover what's happening over there. It disappointed Holly not to visit Egypt and I hope there will be another time for her to do that."

"Yes, but it has to be the right time, Freddie," says Stan, "the librarians will be on their guard for a while, and of course Holly can only come with you when her owners leave her cage unlocked and that doesn't happen often."

"Yes, that's also true," I say. "I feel guilty about Angela, I hope she's not too sad, I think I'd like to see her myself and make sure she's alright, so I'll head over to the vine and then once I know she's OK, I'll go back home and read some books to forget the upset I've caused her."

"That's your choice, Freddie," says Seb, "just don't go inside and stay out of sight, because eventually they'll work out how you're gaining access to the place and close that window."

"Thanks, Seb," I say, "I'll be careful."

With that I bid the crows a fond farewell and wave to Gemma, who is eyeing me with an expression I haven't seen before, one of bemused acceptance.

I canter over to the library where things seem to have calmed down, although the security guard is wiping something gooey from his uniform, obviously a direct hit from the crow Stukas. I work my way up the vine and hang back from the window slightly to overhear any conversations taking place. By the sound of the voices, an important discussion is occurring, so I risk a peek inside the room. Four people are gathered around Angela who is sitting at her desk. My artwork lies on the desk in front of them all – Angela hasn't shredded it yet.

"I don't care what anyone tells me," Angela says, "there's something odd about this photo, the way the two tails are touching is a sign to me, an evil sign, and we need the exorcist to come back and get rid of this phantom cat and rat that disappeared in the men's toilets downstairs."

"They could have jumped out of the window," says a tall gentleman with wavy brown hair I've not seen before.

"How would a rat jump out of a window that's about six feet off the ground?" asks Angela.

"It could have crawled up the wall."

"It's tile-work in there," says the head librarian, "and it's too slippery for animals to grip. A cat might have made it up to the window ledge, but not a rat, so unless the rat's still in there we've no explanation other than an apparition."

"Is anyone searching the toilet?" asks Angela.

"The two male cleaners are looking at everything in there now."

"Could the animals have cooperated?" asks a thin lady called Kirstie who is the receptionist on the first floor, "perhaps the cat gave the rat a lift or a piggy-back up to the window ledge?"

She's got the right idea, I think. *I will have to be wary of her, she's a crafty one.*

"Well, cats and rats don't normally get along," says the head librarian, "so I'm not sure how such cooperation would work. Anyway, we'll get the Reverend Edwards around this time. He removed an evil spirit from my next-door neighbour's shed 2 years ago, so he's effective."

"Why would a ghost haunt a shed?" asks Angela, looking mystified.

"I suppose they have to start somewhere small and work their way up to bigger things, haunting probably takes practice and no little time," suggests the man with the brown hair.

"That's ridiculous," says Angela, "a ghost is a ghost and has no geospatial awareness. I wouldn't have thought they'd feel confined by a shed or be aware of how big it was."

"The ghost cat and rat still ran down the stairs though," according to the customer, which makes me think they weren't ghosts," says Roger, "genuine ghosts wouldn't have to escape; they'd disappear into or through the wall."

"They appear to have done so downstairs, Roger," says the head librarian, "so let's not quibble too much, we'll get the reverend in and see what he can do."

"Yes, Roger, you're trying to throw the cat amongst the pigeons again," says Angela.

The phrase cat amongst the pigeons leads me to think of the book at home by Agatha Christie, the Queen of Mystery Writers. Perhaps it is time to read the book and find out why someone did such a thing to a feline. I have been thrown, and it's not a pleasant experience though it was at a vet and not amongst pigeons, so perhaps my experience was different? Anyway, my concentration is broken and so I thank the people for allowing me to eavesdrop on their conversation, even though they didn't know I was there. I climb down the vine and head back into the house. On the way, I wave to Holly running in her wheel, though not quickly, as though she is tired from her experience earlier in the day.

I climb up the metal staircase acknowledging the Lancashire rose, which is making good progress along the thin wires. I slither in through the window and head downstairs for a poo and a snack. Gemma is asleep in her bed by the window. She is dreaming as her front paws are clasping and unclasping. Her mouth is pulled to one side as though she's in pain. I think about waking her up, to end her possible torment, but then I realise she has to undergo this suffering in order to continue on her life's journey. I feel sorry for her but leave her be.

In the lounge, I find the book *Cat Among the Pigeons* and pull it onto the floor and prepare myself to be mystified by the Queen of Mystery. Well, it's quite exciting because the Middle Eastern country of Ramat is overrun by anti-monarchist revolutionaries and the surviving heir, Princess Shaista, is spirited away to a girls' school called Meadowbank in England. However, various members of staff are killed, and they decide to call Hercule Poirot in to find out what's going on...and that's when I fall asleep.

When I awake, the room is dark apart from the TV. Mary and John are watching a police detective mystery, with Miss Marple in it, another one of the Queen of Mystery's sleuths. How coincidental is that? Well, of course, it isn't. Everything is meant for a reason, but it's odd how these things manifest themselves sometimes. This mystery is called *The Pale Horse* and I decide to watch and discover if I can guess which person is the murderer, but I couldn't. In fact, the person who turns out to be the killer is the only person I never suspect. What does this say about me? Well, that I wouldn't make a good police cat I suppose, if there are such things. Before I can ponder this any further, I fall asleep again, this time on the back of the chair rather than on the floor, and so the sleep lasts a lot longer. At least sleeping is something I am good at.

Chapter 11

Today

I WAKE UP AND FIND it is today again. I search for *Cat Among the Pigeons*, but someone has put the book back on the bookshelf. Well, I can imagine who did that. It was John; he likes a place for everything and everything in its place, but he lost my place in the book by being tidy. Anyway, I remember to meditate on such things, so I imagine sitting cross-legged on a molehill and close my eyes. I feel my breathing regular and deep and satisfying, when guess who comes in and tidies me up by taking me downstairs to eat and poo? Yes, I don't need to tell you, do I? No, I almost miaow in frustration, but I behave myself and remember to treat the kibbles and the litter tray with respect. I also purr when he strokes me, because he's trying to help and not causing me any suffering – indeed he saves me walking down the stairs. Gemma doesn't sneer at me and trots off after eating her breakfast – I'd considered talking to her regarding her dreams, but I didn't want to force things as that might lead to more suffering for both of us. I need to choose the right time and be mature about selecting the opportune moment.

I run up the stairs with some energy and into the kitchen,

where Mary is opening the fridge. There is a large fruit in the centre of the middle shelf – a jackfruit? I worry because the two humans might attack me and Gemma with part of the fruit.

"Are you looking at the watermelon, Freddie?" she asks.

I miaow because I am indeed looking at the watermelon and wondering whether watermelon is a peaceful word for jackfruit. Is there some propaganda going on here?

She takes the fruit out of the fridge and shows it to me. I draw back slightly in case some thuggery ensues, but nothing happens. The fruit smells quite reasonable, so I decide maybe I was wrong, and watermelon means peaceful in fruit language. She smiles and puts the fruit back and I take a quick inventory of what else lives in the fridge, for future reference in case Archimedes ever drops by and helps me lever the door open. I've tried lying on the ground and pawing at the door, but it didn't work, and my legs were too long to fit into the gap between the bottom of the door and the floor, at least in a straight line so I might use them as a lever.

Anyway, she leaves smiling and flourishing her car keys and I scurry into the lounge to read some more of *Cat Among the Pigeons* before intercepting Rufus on his way to the park. In the book, they find another person dead, and I wonder if Agatha, the Queen of Crime, had ever killed all the characters in one of her books by mistake, leaving no one to be the murderer. Except the narrator, perhaps? Could the narrator be the murderer? I will read some more of Agatha's work to find out.

I vacate the premises by the usual method and say a polite 'Good morning' to the rose on the trellis as I manoeuvre down to the grass where there are no crows for a change. Something must be up, maybe in the park? I trot over to the tree. Rufus heads down towards me at a rate of knots. I hope he isn't worried about his nuts.

"You're coming over to the park with me?" he asks.

"Yes, please, if that's OK with you, Rufus?"

"It's fine with me, I'll be glad of the company, but the crows are already over there protecting each other from a small dog that's not on a lead and is chasing them."

"Oh, they'll be indulging in their Blitzkrieg dive-bombing like they were yesterday with a security guard," I reply nonchalantly.

"Well, that sounds like fun, but not for the dog," says Rufus, ambling to a sizeable gap by the side of the road so he can inspect both ways.

I follow him closely as he scurries across the road during a break in the traffic and we head over to the park where the crows are formation flying over a small dog who seems to enjoy the attention. The dog's owner, who should place his canine on a lead, those were the rules according to the sign, is filming the scene using his phone as though it is a documentary on animal behaviour. The dog is barking like dogs do and panting. It's the same man and dog as filmed me 2 days ago.

"How do, Rufus and Freddie," says Ron landing near us, "it's good to welcome you. You're in time to witness us practise our bombing skills on that pesky dog over there, who started chasing Abigail when she was searching for grubs. How dare it do that?"

"The dog should be on a lead according to the sign," I say, indicating the metal pole nearby, "but wait, I might help, because there's a human over there from the city council, according to the uniform, and she looks officious, so I will complain."

"How will you do that?" asks Rufus.

"I will miaow and indicate," I say and scamper off towards the woman who wears an orange bib. I stop close to her and miaow loudly.

She turns and looks at me.

"What is it, kitty cat? Are you alright?"

I miaow, indicate with my head, and take a couple of steps to where the dog is.

"What is it, kitty?"

I miaow for a long time, run off towards the dog, and walk back towards her. She follows my progress and sees the dog being bothered by the crows whose screeching seems to increase suddenly.

"That dog's not on a lead. Is it bothering you, kitty cat? It has certainly upset those crows."

I miaow again – this is getting tiring – and open my eyes wide to appear as though I am pleading, which I am. The dog and the inconsiderate owner are causing unnecessary suffering.

She bustles off towards the dog while bringing out a hand-held device. The crows land in a row and watch.

I head back to Rufus, and we witness a discussion ensue

between the dog owner and the city official, with the official pointing at the dog and the sign. She enters some information in the device, takes a picture of the canine, and prints off a receipt for the owner.

The owner glares at the crows and puts his dog on a lead before marching off towards the children's playground where he sits sulkily on a swing for some seconds before leaving.

"What did you do, Freddie?" asks Abigail.

"I miaowed and alerted her to the situation," I say, "and that's all I could really do. She had to make up her own mind whether she actually did anything. But in her job, people are either vindictive or caring, but either way they want to make a difference and that's what happened. Humans follow some rules and there are certain people who earn a living making sure other humans follow those rules, however inconsequential some people believe those rules to be, and there aren't enough of them sometimes, so when they're around you must make them aware of what's going on, where a rule isn't being followed."

"Right," says Rob, "that was well put, Freddie."

"Thank you, Rob," I say, "I was trying to help, and it seemed to work this time; it doesn't always."

"The question is," says Reg, "whether the owner will remember next time?"

"When the owner receives the demand for payment of the fine, he'll remember, as humans are touchy about money," I reply. "I hope the owner continues to take the dog for a walk and doesn't leave it at home. It's not the dog's fault it's a dog after all, they like barking and being loud, but their enthusiasm gets the better of them and putting them on a lead makes them calm down."

"Yes, that's true about leads and dogs," says Rufus. "I always scamper away when a dog's not on a lead, as they can become nosey sometimes and I don't like that. I reckon they're after my nuts."

"Well," says Rob, "the owner has gone now, so shall we walk around the park?"

"Let's do that," says Rufus, "I would like to try that slide thing, and Freddie would too."

"Yes, and I'd like to go on those swing things," I say, "although I don't possess enough weight to make it move much, because you must build up momentum and there's no one to push me."

"We can all perch on the swing and try to make it move," says Ron, "let's try it."

We head over to the play area, and I jump onto one swing and create some forward momentum. Three crows land on the swing too when it is moving forwards and increase the speed slightly, so that we move higher. Unfortunately, and I never saw this happen, gravity lands on the swing too and pushes me off so that I land in the sand, on all four paws of course. I am annoyed because I was enjoying myself, but gravity spoiled things again. I try to think of a great idea like Isaac did when assaulted by gravity, but nothing comes to mind, which is disappointing. The lady with the orange bib is watching us and might even be filming with her camera, but there is no sign saying cats, crows, and squirrels can't use the playground, so she can't issue us with a ticket and demand for payment, even though I would only pay in kibbles which the authorities wouldn't accept I'm sure. Reg, Rob, and Ron are all on the swing and shouting at me to climb back on, but I want to try the slide again.

I put my paw on the first step and realise my exercises have benefited me, as I can climb up to the top without stopping. I thank the steps for allowing me to climb up them and bow to the slide before moving my tail to the front and shuffling closer to the edge. Suddenly, gravity is there again, but in a good way this time and I head down the slide, leaning backwards slightly so that when I fly off the front, I have a better chance of landing on all four paws. Well, that's what happens, and I like it when a plan comes together. I come back to Earth about four feet away from the end of the slide and then move quickly as Rufus almost lands on top of me. I have another try to propel myself forwards as I leave the slide, which makes about 6 inches of difference in terms of where I land. On the TV, I'd watched humans who take part in a sport called Ski Jumping and observed what techniques they use. Rufus has a problem because he has a bushy tail and this causes what's called a drag in the air, so he can't jump far.

I take a jump at one swing and stay on the seat and gain some momentum. I strain forward trying to get the swing to go higher and I succeed a certain amount, though balancing is difficult. Gravity is busy somewhere else and so I can move backwards and forwards freely. I stick my tail out behind me to help with the streamlining of the surrounding air. I miaow with happiness and see the lady with the orange bib filming me with her phone. Ron and Reg join me on the swing as we glide backwards and forwards, keeping a regular rhythm, until we stop after about 5 minutes.

"That was fun," I say, "it's peaceful rocking backward and forwards like that."

"THAT LADY FROM THE COUNCIL certainly enjoyed our antics," says Reg, "she was smiling away and was definitely filming us, so I wonder what she will do with the footage?"

"Maybe there's a council website where they put films like this, so perhaps she will put her film on the website, though I never go on the Internet, so I won't know."

"Well, if she does and enough people view it, you might become famous, Freddie," says Ron, "celebrity chasing fans will recognise you in the street."

I giggle and see Rufus fall off the end of the slide. He looks tired and takes an age to stand up again. He waves at me and hops away, presumably to get a nut to reinvigorate himself after his exertions.

"What shall we do now?" I ask.

"We can walk around the park and sit on the bench and enjoy the view, though we should wait for young Rufus, who's gone to get a nut. He had about a dozen goes on the slide and tired himself out by the looks of him," says Rob.

"He kept landing in the same place each time, despite all his efforts to get further," says Ron. "Poor thing, it's his tail, it's the opposite of streamlined, he needs it shaving."

"I'm not sure I've ever heard of anyone shaving a squirrel's tail," I say. "The male human shaves, he sprays some white froth out of a tin and then throws it on his face, and then uses a razor to cut off the tiny pieces of hair that have dared to grow on his face. His razor might on a tail."

"Whose tail are you talking about?" asks Rufus, who looks reinvigorated.

"Yours, Rufus," says Rob, "we imagined ways to make you fly in a more streamlined way, so you can jump further off the slide."

"I know, it is my tail, I land in exactly the same place each time despite trying various things to go further, but at least I tried. I tried to go further, but I like my tail, it keeps me warm in the winter, so any trimming would have to be done in the early summer so I can slide on the longer days and then the hair would grow back in the autumn in time for the colder days of winter."

"How would you cut your tail, Rufus?" I ask.

"I've heard of things called scissors," says Rufus, "but I'm not sure where to get them from?"

"They're made for humans," says Abigail, "humans have fingers, strong fingers and thumbs and can operate them safely. It would be the same with a razor. You need strong fingers, not paws, not claws, strong fingers to use one properly."

"That's true," I say, "and I'm not sure the humans can cut Rufus's tail properly, they'd probably shave it and then the hair wouldn't grow back in time for winter and then he'd get cold, and we wouldn't want that."

"If his tail didn't grow back, he might put his tail in a human sock," says Ron, "and then he'd still be warm."

"He might," I say, "and I can get a sock, but we'd probably need to secure it with something because it would fall off when Rufus hopped around."

"And I would hop around," says Rufus, "I keep more active in winter and I keep moving to make sure the blood flows around my body."

"Could you keep your tail in a certain position, so the sock didn't fall off?" asks Rob.

"Climbing up a tree might be more difficult if I had to keep my tail nearly vertical," says Rufus. "I could do it, but I'd be slower."

"How would we convey to the humans that we want them to shave a squirrel's tail?" asks Reg.

I giggle because I'm not sure it would be possible unless we somehow produce pictures of scissors, a tail, and a squirrel to whom the tail belonged. I wonder whether the library would have pictures of items such as these, possibly in the Children's section? If they did, then I'd have to remove them from the library on the strict understanding that I would take them back again afterwards. How does a kitty cat purloin pictures and where would I put them? I'd have to wear something with pockets and then somehow place the cards in the pockets. I'd need an accomplice, or perhaps two?

"What are you pondering, Freddie?" asks Rob.

"I was thinking we can get some cards from the library, perhaps the Children's section, with pictures of scissors and a squirrel on them, and then take them to the humans, and find out whether they would help Rufus."

"They have cards in the library?" asks Abigail.

"I am certain they do. S is for Squirrel, A is for Aircraft, B is for Bird, that sort of thing, C is for Cat, with a picture next to the letter."

"Squirrel, I can understand, but would they have a picture of scissors?" asks Rufus.

"Well, perhaps not, but maybe they'd have pictures of a knife or a sword?"

"But we wouldn't want to give them the wrong impression. What would happen if they understood you wanted to turn Rufus into a kebab?" asks Ron.

"What's a kebab?" I ask.

"It's meat on a sharp stick or skewer, which they burn slightly before eating," says Reg, "and tastes strange."

"Oh no, no, that would be terrible. Perhaps there'd be a picture of a razor?" I suggest.

"You'd have to discover what is there," says Jacqueline, who's just arrived, "but are you sure there are such cards in the library, I don't remember seeing anything like that?"

"I've seen some cards or a book with letters of the alphabet in it, where there was a letter and then a representation of a figure beginning with that letter."

"I'll have a peek through the window this afternoon," replies Jacqueline, "because the kids' section is on the ground floor at the back, so you can stay there for ages. I will find out if I can spot any cards or books as you describe them."

"Thank you, Jacqueline," I say. "That would be most useful. If there are no such cards, then I'm not sure how we will make Rufus more aerodynamic."

"I'm not sure it's worth it," says Rufus. "Although it would be nice to fly like an airplane, all streamlined, and smooth, I'm not sure it's worth feeling cold for during the whole winter."

"Only you can decide the priorities," says Rob, "but we can still try to find those cards for you, to see what options there are."

"We could try I suppose," says Rufus, "but it would be difficult, even if the cards were there, wouldn't it, Freddie?"

"It would be a challenge," I reply, "especially removing the cards without any human noticing. I'd have to carry them in my mouth or in a pocket of a garment, but I can't remember anything I could wear that would fit me and allow me to carry cards and then there's the problem of pushing the cards into the pocket. Carrying in the mouth sounds better."

"There's a window in that children's area," says Jacqueline, "which is sometimes open slightly, but not enough for you to climb through. Might you throw the cards through the window and then we could pick them up and fly off with them?"

"I was thinking more of other people being around and watching us take the cards and not doing anything," says Rufus. "I mean they're humans so they will not watch as Freddie looks through some cards and then throws them out of the window, they're going to stop him, and possibly capture him."

"We'll have to have a diversion," I say, "something that distracts the human children and their parents for a suitable amount of time so we can search through the cards – because I will need some help – and select the most appropriate ones before throwing out of the window or running out of the library with them in my mouth."

"How about a bomb threat?" says Abigail.

"What? How would we organise that?" asks Ron. "We'd need a human to phone the library on our behalf."

"We might play a recording of someone saying it on a TV program or from a film," says Rufus, "though I'm not sure where we'd get a recording device from, and we'd have to learn how to play the recording at the appropriate time."

"Wouldn't it be better to create a diversion or go into the library when children wouldn't be there, such as at lunch or later in the evening?" says Rob.

"We should do some research," says Jacqueline, "perhaps there's a time when no one is there. I can check every 30 minutes to see how many people there are."

"Thank you," I say. "That would be really useful, let's hope there's a period when we can operate undetected."

"Where are the cards, Freddie?" asks Rufus.

"When I saw them they were on the table on the ground floor," I reply.

"I'll check that," says Jacqueline. "They sometimes place items in a drawer in the table, but the kids take them out as soon as they arrive."

"This is all good information," I say, "but the fundamental problem is going to be getting to the children's area. We could go in via the men's toilet and then scamper along the corridor before turning left. We'll be awfully exposed when running along the corridor and out into the main part of the library."

"A pleasant diversion by the front door would be in order," says Ron, "just enough, so that everyone is looking the wrong way for a few seconds."

"That would be useful and then we'd have to have another diversion when we'd finished so we can scuttle back or perhaps push through the window in the children's area if it's open."

"I reckon they lock that window in place," says Jacqueline, "but I can check to make sure."

"Thank you," I say. "Anyway, we should sit on the bench, because the lady with the bright bib has been filming us with her camera."

We head uphill towards the top of the park and congregate around the bench – 1 cat, 1 squirrel, and 5 crows. Seb, Stan, and Sid soon spot us, so the bench becomes crowded.

"Hello, everyone, hello Freddie and Rufus," says Stan. "How are you all today? You're going to be famous. The lady from the council was filming you and smiling, so I wonder which website you'll be on?"

"All of them, Stan," I reply. "All of them. We might need your help. We were discussing how we could trim Rufus's tail so he becomes more aerodynamic and flies better off the slide and we thought we'd ask my humans to trim his tail by borrowing some cards from the library with pictures on so they can take the hint."

"It wouldn't be like humans to take the hint," says Seb, "they're not that bright sometimes."

Everyone laughs at this remark.

"Yesterday," says Sid, "some of them were sitting in their cars on the big road over there for 2 hours waiting for a large lorry type vehicle to move and none of them ever got out, they just sat there, looking at their mobile devices."

"Mobile devices for when you're immobile," says Seb.

Again, we all giggle.

"There's a dog over there," says Rufus.

"Is it pulling its owner along behind it?" asks Abigail.

"It is, it's the same owner as last time we were sitting on this bench," says Rufus.

"That's not good," I say. "Her name's Penny, and she knows my humans as last time she visited us she told them about my visit to the park, but I looked innocent, and they didn't believe her, but she might try to get photographic evidence, so I will try to hide until she has passed."

"We can do our Junkers JU-87 Stuka impression, if you like," says Reg, "and get rid of her that way?"

"No, let's not cause her any further suffering," I say. "I'll hide in the rhododendron until she's gone."

"How do you know she's suffering?" says Jacqueline. "She looks happy to me walking with her little dog, she's very content."

"All humans are suffering," I say, "but most don't realise or deny it or do nothing about it until it's too late or do something bad and then when they're reincarnated they come back as an insect or a dog or a primrose."

"Do we eat former unhappy humans, Freddie?" asks Seb. "Because that might explain why I get indigestion sometimes when I've eaten a juicy worm."

I smile because I'm not 100% certain whether I know the answer to that question, as I haven't read specifically whether unhappiness or suffering can pass on to others after reincarnation.

"I don't know the answer for sure, Seb," I say. "I will have to read one of my books on Buddhism to find that out. What I reckon, is that karma's considered a mental act or intention. Having formed the intention, you perform acts by speech, mind, and body, and these can either be wholesome or unwholesome. If they're wholesome, then you're reincarnated in the happy realms, but if the actions are unwholesome, then it's the unhappy realms for you, so when you eat a worm then there's no knowing whether the worm is in the happy or unhappy realms, it depends on their previous existence. However, the happiness or the unhappiness wouldn't be passed on to any creature that ate the worm as that wouldn't be fair to that creature, as your karma is based on your deeds in this life not on someone else's deeds in their previous lives. You can't interrogate everything you eat before you eat it to find out what it did in previous lives and then decide what to do based on any answer you receive, not that worms can communicate in a way we can understand."

"Right," says Seb, "that seems fair. I'm glad I control my karma."

"Penny is getting closer, so I will lurk in the rhododendron bush for a few seconds until she's gone," I say, and jump down. I hide under a low branch and monitor her as she comes into view. The crows gather around Rufus, who puts on his best cute squirrel's face as Penny approaches. She doesn't seem surprised that the crows just watch her as she comes nearer. She takes out her phone and taps the screen twice before adopting a stealthier approach with the phone in front of her. The crows part to reveal Rufus, who turns around and lifts his tail up in the air. This is a vulgar thing to do, of course, and from a Buddhist point of view I don't approve, but part of me can't help giggling. Penny stares for a few seconds before looking under the bench and then around about. The crows hop onto the back of the bench to show a scene with no cat visible. She puts her phone away, turns around, and slopes off towards the edge of the park, leading her little dog. I watch as she heads away and feel sorry for her as she would suffer, although I have to remind myself that it is partly her fault for building up her own expectations which have not been fulfilled. It is up to her to learn a life's lesson from this scene. Sometimes you expect a cute cat but get a squirrel's backside instead. That's life. I watch Penny depart and then jump back onto the bench.

"I like your choreography the coordinated parting of the ways to reveal a squirrel's bum," I say. "I hope she learned her lesson not to raise her expectations too much too soon."

"It's not the sort of video she'll post on her Facebook page," says Rob, "unless she's hoping to surprise people. She'd have to put a warning at the beginning."

"She was hoping to video me and then show my humans what a wayward cat they have, a cat who crosses the road, and associates with wildlife," I say, "and that's not a nice thing to do – I mean, it's not her business after all."

"You're right, Freddie, but unfortunately I have to inspect

my caches and then head back over the road. Are you coming with me?" Rufus sounds impatient.

"Yes, will do, Rufus. What's the next step as regards the visit to the library?"

"I'll let you know what I find out this afternoon regarding visitors in the children's area and about the cards," says Jacqueline. "Where will you be in your house if I need to tell you something later?"

"I'll be in the lounge either reading a book or asleep on the back of the couch."

"Right, I'll tap on the window nearest the couch."

"That's excellent, thank you, Jacqueline," I say, and jump down with Rufus. "Thank you all, I will see you soon. Take care, everyone."

The crows caw their goodbyes in unison and I'm sure any human listening would think they are unhappy about something, but they aren't. Rufus visits the trees in a certain order and seems satisfied that his nuts are all present and correct. I glance around to see whether anyone is filming us, but few people are around. The weather is warm, and some bits of blue sky lie overhead, so more people might come into the park later. Rufus finds a suitable gap in the traffic, and we run across the road to his tree.

"When you go to the library to get the cards, if there are some, can I come too?"

"Yes, Rufus, I will need some help. A pair of keen eyes will be most welcome. I wonder if Holly can come along also, because she didn't have time to visit Egypt when we were there last."

"That sounds great, thank you, I will look forward to that. I hope your humans will trim my tail properly and that they get the message."

"Well," I say, "I don't wish to worry you, Rufus, but humans don't cut their own hair, they go to barbers or hairdressers who cut it for them, so most humans never practice the art of haircutting."

"Don't the males shave their hair?" asks Rufus, twitching slightly.

"They do on their faces and sometimes under their arms in what's called the armpit, but usually in a mirror. On their face the hair isn't very long, it seems like an overreaction to me, the hairs are barely visible, Rufus."

"Would you trust them to cut the fur on your tail?" says Rufus.

"My fur is a lot shorter on my tail than it is on your tail, Rufus, so it's not the same at all, but no I wouldn't, not with a pair of scissors."

I pat Rufus's tail with my paw and feel how fluffy it is. It appears about 75% of the thickness of the tail is fur, which is why he isn't very aerodynamic. I am glad my tail isn't like that because it must be like walking around attached to a toilet brush.

"OK, well, I will have to trust them because I want to go further on that slide," replies Rufus. "Anyhow, I should go, and I expect to hear from you soon."

"Yes, I wouldn't worry too much about the tail trimming until we have found suitable cards and exited the library. It will not be straightforward to do that. There might not be any suitable cards and the library might capture us, so we shouldn't take anything for granted until we're back safely in the garden and have worked out how to show the cards to the humans and where."

"Thank you, Freddie, see you soon," he replies and runs up the trunk of the tree.

I climb in through the kitchen window and trot downstairs for a respectful snack in the basement before continuing to read *Cat Among the Pigeons* in the lounge. So far, no cat has appeared in the book and no pigeons either and I feel I can't rely on Agatha to provide a meaningful title for a book. Another person has been murdered though, which makes me glad we don't live near a school, because they sound dangerous places especially their sports halls and locker rooms. I can't work out who's done the deed and wonder whether all the characters might have done it together or whether Agatha has ever written a book where that has happened. With this idea playing through my head, I fall asleep only to be woken by a tapping on the window.

My eyes open and I see Jacqueline waving at me to come outside. I stretch and then scuttle across the floor into the kitchen and out through the window. I climb down the trellis and trot to the front of the house, where Jacqueline awaits.

"Hello, Freddie," she says, "sorry to wake you up but there's something you should see in the library in the Children's section."

"Oh good," I say, "and I was just dozing really, because I don't remember dreaming at all."

"Let's go to the back of the library. I will see you there in a minute, there's some people around so you might have to go through the undergrowth to remain out of sight."

I giggle as Jacqueline flies off. I jump onto the gate and assess the situation. There are indeed several people standing around the door, as though waiting for something to happen or for someone to arrive. I decide to run along the fence and then jump into the library garden, where the flowers and low bushes will shield me from view, which I thank them for. I emerge onto the pavement and trot around to the window where Jacqueline is perched, looking inside. The small window is open slightly and I jump up to inspect.

"What's happening, Jacqueline, it looks like people are expecting an important visitor?"

"There's something going on," she replies, "but before we get distracted, there was no one in this area for about 30 minutes between 12:45 and 1:15. It was as though they were all at lunch."

"Oh, it's because there has to be a librarian present at all times and that person has to have a lunch break to feed themselves. Of course, why didn't I realise that? They don't feed themselves at the desk where they work, they feed themselves somewhere else."

"Well, that's good news. Now the next thing is to look at the table."

"The book of ABC animals, oh such as C for Cat, D for Dog?"

"That's right, and there are also some cards with a big letter in the top-left corner with a picture of an animal, they're scattered on the floor, and there's definitely one for squirrel, S for Squirrel, I saw it and the squirrel has a big tail."

"That's good."

"There are similar books for the kitchen and for food, so perhaps there might be some cards for them too."

"I could look through the books to see whether there's a suitable picture of a cutting implement."

"There might be a K for Knife in the food book."

"Thank you, Jacqueline. Oh, look, who is that?"

"That's the vicar, Freddie, he'll be doing the exorcism upstairs in Angela's office."

"I see, well if everyone is distracted, I wonder if I can paw this window open any wider?" I suggest. I try to stick my chin in the gap, but it gets stuck, and I have to wiggle myself free. I place my paw in the gap and attempt to move the window, but without success. The window appears to be stuck. Once again Archimedes isn't around with a helpful lever to open the window, just one inch wider. I look at the window and see the handle and push at that.

"You push from the other side, Freddie, so try pulling," suggests Jacqueline.

I see her point, but I don't really have many muscles for pulling, plus my paw keeps slipping off the metal, but I persevere and endure some failure before moving the handle slightly and opening the window a little, just enough for me to stick my chin through. If I can get my chin through a gap, I know the rest of me can get through too. Cats have whiskers to measure gaps and when their whiskers encounter resistance, then they know they have to shove with their chin, that's how it works. This movement of the handle encourages me and suggests if I were inside, I could move the handle, open the window, and leave along with any other animals that were with me. Suddenly a human voice says,

"Look, there's the apparition, at the window. Get the reverend now and let him banish it."

I am not sure who said that, but in a minute the vicar comes into view and holds up a cross in my direction and says a prayer. He is a tall man with grey hair and prominent black eyebrows.

"You should quickly disappear," says Jacqueline, "as though you're a ghost that vanishes without a trace."

"That sounds like a good idea," I reply. "Oh, he's walking towards me now and brandishing the cross at me."

"I'm going to walk along the ledge and then fly off."

Underneath the window are some low bushes. I glance down and see a suitable landing spot, and then look back through the window as Jacqueline flaps her wings and disappears without a sound. The man is halfway towards me from his original starting point; it is time to exit. I miaow in his direction in what I hope would appear to be a generous gesture and then step backwards off the ledge, land on my paws, and then scamper to a hiding place as I feel sure he will open the window.

The reverend does indeed open the window to look around outside and, satisfied the ghostly presence has disappeared, he withdraws his head but leaves the window open.

I wonder whether this is a trap to determine whether the cat is real or a ghost, because a normal cat, a non-Freddie cat, would probably be curious about why the window is open and return, only to be pounced upon by a sceptical librarian and held up for ridicule by the library readers. I determine to be cleverer than that and slink away, sight unseen, towards the house. The crows are cawing, so I take stock of my position before breaking cover and jumping over the fence into my garden, where I can breathe easily again.

Abigail and Jacqueline land close to me.

"You're a smart cat," says Abigail, "the head librarian was waiting to see whether you'd appear at the window and might still be there right now. The vicar reckons he's got rid of you, the ghostly apparition, but some of the staff aren't so sure."

"I wondered," I reply, "and it's better to err on the side of discretion than be captured and so be unable to help my friend Rufus have his tail shaped by a pair of scissors."

"What confused them was that there was no rat with you this time, so they're wondering what happened to the rat and whether it's still inside the library," says Jacqueline.

"Oh, poor Holly, I'm not sure I should tell her that the library calls her a rat, but I'm going to need her help when we get those cards and maybe the book."

"The three of you will be conspicuous, Freddie," says Abigail, "so we'll have to provide some enjoyable diversions for you at the right times."

"Yes, I'll probably have to take Holly to the Egypt books as well, as she's been looking forward to seeing pictures of the Pyramids for years. Rufus is not interested in Egypt."

"Rufus is probably going to be interested in Brazil where

the nuts come from, so you might have to do without both of them for part of your escapade," says Jacqueline.

"That could be difficult, especially if someone sees either of them. They won't know what to do with themselves."

"Could you bring Gemma along?" says Jacqueline. "She'd keep them under control."

"Well, she might eat them both if they didn't cooperate or swat them unconscious, which is not what I want for either Rufus or Holly really, but it might not be the worst thing that could happen to them, especially if the humans caught them."

"What would happen if she knocked them out?" asks Abigail.

"She'd carry them out in her mouth, probably one at a time," I say, cringing at the prospect. "Anyway, we'll cross that bridge if we come to it. She's unpredictable."

"Well, we are trying to help Rufus ultimately," says Abigail, "so he should really cooperate with us."

"Rufus will cooperate, but Holly's primary motivation will be to see pictures of Egypt, which is on a different floor, that might be problematic."

"What are your plans for getting the cards and perhaps the book in front of the humans and making them understand what you want them to do?" asks Jacqueline.

"Well, I was going to place the cards on the floor and then ask Rufus to appear and then place the card with the scissors on his tail."

"Well, that's getting to the point, isn't it?" says Abigail.

"It is, but you can't afford to be subtle with them, because they won't understand, you have to be firm and decisive.

Humans like to be shown what to do or at least believe they've been decisive themselves in some particular way, even if we make hints about their future behaviour."

"You sound very organised, Freddie," says Abigail, "have you had much practice at this?"

"Not much, but it's not manipulative if you're trying to help other people with relief from their suffering and you can't help them yourself but know someone who can help them, even if that person doesn't know it. If I can see this is happening, it's behoven of me to help. I'd feel awful if I did nothing and a person or animal remained unhelped or unhappy and suffered."

"I see," says Jacqueline, "but we should help each other all the time, shouldn't we?"

"Yes, we should, you're correct, Jacqueline, but you assume you can always tell when someone needs help, and that's not always the case. Sometimes you have to sense it and then find out whether something is bothering that animal."

"So you could tell Rufus was upset that he couldn't jump very far off the slide because of the dragging effect of his thick, bushy tail?"

"Yes, he was getting droopy and staring at his tail and shaking his head. He was an unhappy squirrel and needed some hope that some judicious streamlining of his tail could make things better. He soon perked up when he had some idea he could improve his flying skills."

"What happens if his tail is trimmed, and he doesn't fly as far as he reckons he should?" asks Abigail.

"Well, we can't do anything about that, really," I say. "His expectations have to be realistic. Perhaps he'll be able to fly another foot or 18 inches with a trimmed tail, who knows. After that, he might want to wear something that makes him even more streamlined, in which case we should talk to him about his situation and why he appears to have this obsession, but we should cross that bridge if we come to it."

"That sounds very caring, Freddie," says Jacqueline. "You're a good friend to Rufus, and you seem to know a lot about him. I thought all he wanted was to collect as many nuts as possible."

"He still does," I reply, smiling, "but perhaps he now realises there's more to life than that. Who knows what motivates him? Anyway, I should get back inside because the humans will be back soon, and I want to get some more reading done. I will see you soon."

"Bye, Freddie," say the crows as they fly off to the park.

I amble over to the trellis and wish the Lancashire Rose a pleasant afternoon as I haul myself up the metal to the window. Suddenly, thoughts come into my mind, "Good afternoon, young cat, I wish you well for the rest of the day, I wish I could climb as fast as you do." I stare down at the rose and wonder what just happened.

"You understand me?" I say.

The leaves of the rose rustle in unison, though the rest of the garden is still.

I close my eyes and try to transmit a thought, but I'm not sure how to direct it to the rose as it covers a large area and I'm not sure which part of it does the communicating.

"I'm sending you a thought," I say, "it's lovely to meet

you Lancashire rose and I hope you climb as far as you want to."

The leaves again move as if in understanding. I stare at the rose for a few seconds but appear not to receive another message.

I trot into the lounge and continue to read *Cat Among the Pigeons* with its cast of strong female characters, contrasting them in my mind with *The Sign of Four* by Conan Doyle, who only seems to have female characters to create plotlines. The humans come home so I pretend to be asleep, but make sure the book is underneath the sofa where I can read it later when they are watching TV and not suspecting their cat is reading a book.

After eating and a poo, I am back under the sofa when there is a knock on the front door. The murderers are about to be revealed when Mary shows Penny into the lounge. Penny is on her own and clutching something in her right hand, something that looks like her phone.

"I saw your Freddie cat in the park again today. I'm sure it's him. He was fraternising with the crows and jumping on the swings. Here's a video of him, although it's taken from too far away to identify him properly. When I tried to creep up on him when he was sitting on the bench with the squirrel and the crows, he disappeared."

"Did he?" says John with what can be called scepticism heaped on irony with large doses of doubt.

"Can we look at the video?" says Mary.

Penny shows the video to them while I marvel at Hercule's powers of deduction especially about girls' knees.

"As you say, Penny, it's certainly far away," says Mary.

"It is a cat though," says John, "with some black and white markings who is the centre of attention. That squirrel seems obsessed with the slide, but its tail is dragging him down. Poor thing, he isn't designed to fly. He always lands in the same place, but he is very persistent."

My ears perk up when I hear this. Some sympathy for the squirrel? Already? Perhaps shearing some fur from his tail will be easy to achieve. We just have to get the scissors, the human, the squirrel, and the inclination to help in the same place at the same time. But at least John is acquainted with Rufus's problem and can understand why the tail trimming has to be done.

"Do you recognise Freddie?" asks Penny.

"Well, can you enlarge the image?" asks Mary.

Penny swipes away at the screen while I reconcile how Agatha could have two murderers in one book. Working out which person is the killer is difficult, but two makes it unfair.

"It looks a bit like Frederick," says John, which alerts me to something. I'd noticed he uses my full name when he thinks I've done something not good and so now I will have to look innocent for the rest of the evening, "but it's not conclusive is it? It's definitely not Gemma, because she wouldn't be so popular and would try to swat all those other animals as they were getting too close. But it can't be Freddie as he can't get out of the house during the day and he's always here when we get home in the evening."

I nod my head at that last sentiment.

"He knew he was being filmed," says Penny, "and hid before I got too close. I'm amazed that the crows and the squirrel didn't appear frightened by my presence, they let me get very close."

"There are quite a few humans in that park at all times, and the animals are probably used to the contact," replies John. "That's all it is."

"Oh wait, there was someone else there, from the council. She had a high-res jacket on, and Freddie complained to her about a dog not being on a lead. She filmed Freddie on the swing, I'm sure. I will contact the council about that. Your cat has hidden talents and a secret life when you're out at work."

"Well, seeing is believing," says Mary, in her usual reasonable tone. "Anyway, would you like a glass of wine, Penny, we've got a bottle of white chilling in the fridge?"

"I'd love a glass of wine," replies Penny, already heading in the direction of the kitchen. This pleases me no end as she is obviously a close observer of my behaviour and I wonder whether I should wear a disguise when I go over to the park again, though I'm not sure what. I've never seen V for Vendetta masks for cats, but I should keep my eyes open. They're also called Guy Fawkes masks. I might have to wear a cape too, or a small coat to cover my fur, as a face mask wouldn't be sufficient disguise for a furry animal such as myself. I have markings on my fur, which are like fingerprints for humans and distinguish me from other cats.

Anyway, with the *Cat Among the Pigeons* book not containing a single feline and no birds to speak of, I decide to have a rest from Agatha and try a travel writer named Bill Bryson who has written a book called *In A Sunburned Country* which was down under some other books on the bottom shelf. I remove it with some swift swipes of my front paws, only to find a picture on the front of a monstrous creature, which has another creature struggling to escape from its stomach. This is not appealing, but according to Bill, Australia has a lot of dangerous animals, so I might have to be careful when walking past the Australia section in the library.

It is with this happy thought that I wander off into a cheerful sleep where I dream about spelling out various words using the cards I am going to borrow from the library. The only problem is that some words are considered rude and offend the neighbours – Fascist being one example and Jackfruit another. The neighbours are convinced I am directing the words at them and complain to the police. A short Belgian detective with a large moustache comes to the house and threatens to prosecute the humans for causing offence and for having boring knees. The humans' excuse that it is the cat who's spelled out the words is not accepted as believable, but then some pigeons come and steal the cards and take them back to the library. All this happens to the backdrop of a squirrel winning the world ski-flying title after having his tail styled by a world-famous hairdresser, so the squirrel is aerodynamically perfect, flying like an arrow over the ground.

Chapter 12

Today

TODAY IS THE NEXT DAY I want to write about. The 2 previous days were the weekend when the humans don't go to work and get paid, but do lots of work around the house, such as washing, cleaning, and tidying up the mess they create during the week. They also wake up later than they do during the week, and this is a concern for me as I like to be fed at the same time every day so that my digestive system knows it will process the food at the same time each day and can plan accordingly.

On Sunday, my digestive system is complaining that it's food-processing time and there's no food in my bowl. Therefore, I try to find the humans. Apparently, according to a note in the kitchen, she's gone for a walk with friends in the trees somewhere and he's asleep making loud snorting sounds from his mouth and nose. Well, it's a terrible sound and shows me his air passages are blocked. To be honest, it sounds like he is suffering, so I'm in a quandary, because I should relieve him of his suffering, but he is asleep and entitled to his relaxation. I am hungry though, so I decide the best thing to do is to help him wake up without causing him to become awake, make it a gradual transition rather than a sudden reflex action. My solution is more of a molehill solution than a mountain solution. He is splayed on the bed under a sheet and also making noises from hidden orifices, showing that not all passages are blocked. I would open the window to let some fresh air in if I could.

First, I jump onto the bed and then jump off again to discover if this gentle impact would make any difference. It doesn't; he breathes loudly through his nose like a small steam train starting out from a station. I've seen this once on a TV program and it sounded like a lot of effort went into propelling the train in a forward direction. It mystifies me how the male human is making so much noise with so little effort and no one is feeding him coal. I jump up again and pat his moustache with my paw, touching the hairs under his nose. He breathes through his mouth, although it is more like blowing, as though he is trying to get rid of my paw. But at least he's stopped sounding like a steam train. I move and slide my paw along the hairs on his moustache in a sideways motion, causing him to move his lips around and emit a 'nerrrrrrrrrrrrrr' sound. This is not a word I'm familiar with, but when I remove my paw the snoring starts again. I try rubbing his prominent black eyebrows, but this has no effect other than to make the choo-choo train start again. Then, I hit upon the idea of patting his nose with my paw, but this only causes wrinkling of the nose and no discernible change in his breathing. I place my paw on his nose and move it around, but this means he hisses through his mouth. I am at a loss.

"That's all been very laudable, Freddie and very kind,

caring, and Buddhist but not effective," says Gemma behind me. "I should try, and I would advise you to stand by the door."

"Why? What are you going to do?" I ask.

"I'm going to wake him up by smacking him on his snout," she replies, "in about 10 seconds, so I would vacate the premises, Freddie."

I jump down onto the carpet and go out of the room, but I peer round the door to view proceedings.

Gemma jumps onto the bed, positions herself carefully, draws back her right paw, and swats John right on the nose. His eyes fly open as Gemma flees the scene. I walk over to the lounge and continue to read my book until I hear him stumbling around in the bathroom. Eventually, about 3 hours later than normal, he pokes his head around the lounge door and says, "Breakfast, Freddie."

I miaow and follow him downstairs, having noticed he has some red marks on his nose, which aren't from me, of course.

Gemma is eating heartily as I conduct my pre-breakfast routine in the litter tray and in front of the food bowl.

Gemma finishes before me and then says, "He doesn't know it was me who woke him up. He reckons he was dreaming and woke up with a start because of something in his dream."

"You dream, Gemma," I say. "Did you know that?"

"Do I?" she says. "How do you know?"

"I witnessed you when you were asleep a few days ago and your whiskers were twitching and you were baring your teeth, by pulling back your lips."

She sits down and puts her tail around her paws.

"I do dream, Freddie, but they're vague in my memory when I wake up. They usually involve my kittens being taken away from me, all four of them, they didn't leave me with one, but that's normally all I can remember."

"I'm sorry that happened to you, Gemma," I say. "I didn't know. It must be terrible to lose your children like that."

"It is, humans are so callous and cruel about these things, they don't understand we cats have feelings, and that we're not just kitten breeding machines who can soon get more kittens if we lose the ones we've just given birth to. Anyway, thank you for letting me talk about this, it's difficult for me as you can probably imagine. I enjoyed swatting the human, but I know it's not his fault. I just take my anger out on him as he's an embodiment of the humanity I despise."

"But he's not the one who took your kittens away, is he? He's quite kind really, well they both are."

"They are both nice in their own ways, I suppose," says Gemma, "you are right, Freddie, but it's difficult to get over an injustice."

"I miss my mum," I reply. "They took me away from her when I was young, and I often wonder where she is and how she is, and I realise I'll never know. She could live close by, and I'll never know, but I think about her and hope that she's thinking of me wherever she is, and I hope she's happy and content and not having to go through what you're going through."

"I hope so too, Freddie. What is her name?"

"Her name is Emma, strangely enough, not so different

from your name, and I have a sister called Daisy, but she was taken away too at the same time as me. I wonder if I met my mum, whether she'd remember me?"

Gemma smiles and stands up. "You needn't worry about that, Freddie; your mum will never forget you and would recognise you even though you've undoubtedly changed a lot and grown a lot since she last saw you."

==========

AS YOU CAN SEE FROM the previous today, or yesterday as it's called in the human world, Gemma and I had a pleasant conversation about her dreams and my mum and where she might be today. I felt a lot better afterwards and hoped Gemma did, too. It was almost as though we were on the same side at last. It had been a very enjoyable day overall.

Things improve even further when I observe through the window that Holly is running in her wheel towards the park – her owners didn't lock the cage again, so we can go to the library and Holly may visit Egypt while Rufus and I search for alphabetic cards and books around the children's area. I must make sure Rufus knows before he goes over to the park and that the crows are aware too, so they can help move the cards and create a diversion if necessary.

As is often the way when you're waiting for something to happen, time seems to drag and the humans take forever to go to work, even though they always leave at the same time according to the clock in the kitchen. I am reading my book on Australia in which Bill explains how a gold prospector lost a complete gold field because he had to return to base to get some more equipment. I bet that was frustrating as gold is a valuable commodity to humans though it's not much use to cats, but then again neither is silver nor platinum. I like tin the best because it contains cat food, and that's good for cats.

Anyway, the humans leave, and I depart, noting that the window seems slightly wider than normal or maybe I am getting thinner? I don't seem thinner, but maybe there's more muscle now and I am more toned and sleeker.

I gallop over to Holly's window and confirm that she wants to go to the library today at 12:30pm and that we'll enter via the librarian's window and exit via the window in the children's area. Holly is happy with this idea and looks forward to seeing Egypt. I leave her in a joyful state, run around her garden fence for exercise, and talk to Jacqueline and Seb in the garden. I tell them what our plans are, assuming Rufus can come to the library, of course. They fly off to get things organised on their side of things, which judging by the resulting cawing is plenty.

Rufus comes down from his tree at 9:55am precisely. I ask him whether he can go to the library today at 12:30pm. He replies he will be ready and will meet me at the base of his tree at 12:25pm. If we'd owned watches, we'd have synchronised them as they do in some spy books, but we don't own watches, so I rely on the clock in the house. We agree on what we'll do when we are inside because we must be decisive and make the best use of our time. Rufus understands as he wants to fly in a streamlined manner from the base of the slide and his tail needs to be a lot less bushy.

I scout around the library, checking that everything appears normal, and that the librarian's upstairs window is open and the window by the children's area is too. I trot back home and decide to read a book called *The Plague* by Albert Camus, about an outbreak of pestilence in a place called Oran in Algeria set in 194-. I wonder when 194- is because it's not a year I recognise. Is it before 1940 i.e., 1940-1? I'm not sure because I understood 1940-1 would be 1939. Anyway, Albert's book is a work of fiction but sounds plausibly scary because there's a huge die-off of rats at the beginning and then the humans die too. If I find a dead rat, then I will get worried about my humans and hope they're OK. Having said that, I understand the disease passes from rat to human via a carrier or vector and as no self-respecting rat would ever come near our house because of Gemma, then Mary and John should be safe.

At 12:20pm I scuttle out of the window and down the trellis, saying good afternoon to the rose, who has made noticeable progress since the morning. A thought of, "Good afternoon, young Freddie," arrives in my mind. I collect Holly from her house, and we head over to Rufus's tree. He runs down to meet us, and we start off towards the library. The plan is for us to enter via the librarian's window, not create art on the photocopier machine, head down to the Travel section where we'll leave Holly, so she can stare at pictures of Egypt for 30 minutes, before Rufus and I go to the Children's section. We'll pass the cards or book through the window before I fetch Holly and we'll leave through the same window.

That is the plan.

We trot over to the library, keeping in the shadows. Holly is riding on my back again, and Rufus tries hard not to giggle.

"If the humans see you two, they'll invent a new sport which they can bet on," he says as we sneak through the undergrowth towards the vine.

"You're right, Rufus," says Holly, "but they'd need to invent some small reins and a bridle for cats, so we could make them go faster."

I smile as I climb the vine towards the window. We arrive at the ledge. There is no librarian, as she has gone home for lunch to walk her dogs. We clamber through the window and before I can stop him, Rufus creates some art on the photocopier. He has a manic look in his eye, and I realise he already knows how to operate the machine. Holly makes sure the coast is clear in the corridor. I hit the silver disk on the wall with my back paws, just to show off. The door yawns ajar and we scuttle to the right and down the stairs to the Travel section. Holly scrambles on board again, and I jump up to Egypt. We find three books with lots of pictures, and I wedge them open so Holly can paw through them in her own time. She's thrilled and overcome by the grandeur and splendour of the temples and tomb paintings.

"I'll be back in about 30 minutes, Holly," I say, but Holly has travelled back in time already and doesn't hear me.

Rufus and I wait until a visitor moves from the Travel section before we head downstairs towards the Children's section, which appears to be free of people. Abigail and Jacqueline are by the window. Abigail flies off and Jacqueline hops towards the open window. I turn towards the front door, where a commotion starts. As people look towards the noise, Rufus and I scamper over to the table and jump up. I head to the window where I push at the handle, so that the window opens enough to let me through. That is our escape route sorted out, now to find the cards and the book.

"Freddie," says Rufus, "I've found a book of the alphabet for animals."

We scan through it and sure enough there is a page, S for Squirrel. I pick up the book in my mouth and push it through the gap in the window and it falls into the bush, where I can pick it up later, as it would be too heavy for the crows to fly with.

"There are plenty of cards, but nothing for scissors," says Rufus.

I find some food and kitchen cards and there is one entitled K for Knife.

"This will do," I say, pushing the card through the window, where Jacqueline grabs it and flies off.

"There's nothing else," says Rufus, "other than a P for Pirate, where the pirate has a sword."

"Brilliant," I say. "I can point at the sword and then point at your tail."

I bite the card and push it through the gap, where Abigail picks it up and heads away.

"What's going on?" says a human voice.

Rufus stands still and looks at the human. I am closer to the window and observe Rufus is transfixed. I grab his tail and drag him across the table. He turns around and heads through the window, closely followed by me. I pick up the book and run as fast as I can round the library. The crows start another commotion near the entrance, and I jump over the fence into my garden undetected. I place the book under the front steps, out of sight of any human. Now, the only problem is that we need a rescue mission to get Holly, who is still in Egypt.

Jacqueline and Abigail arrive, along with their cards, which I place with the book. Reg, Ron, and Rob soon join us.

"There is a problem," I say. "Holly is still inside, and we need to rescue her as soon as possible, otherwise she might be captured."

"What happened inside?" asks Abigail.

"A human shouted at us," says Rufus, "and we had to scarper otherwise we would have been trapped and captured and who knows what might have happened."

"It would have been embarrassing to be captured," I say, "but I shouldn't leave Holly behind like that, she'll be scared."

"Here's trouble," says Rob, "your friend Gemma is out of the house."

I turn around and sure enough, Gemma is walking slowly towards us. About 3 yards away, she stops and says, "There seems to be a problem. May I approach and try to help?"

"Yes, please come closer, Gemma," I say. She approaches and sits upright, putting her tail over her paws. I explain the situation.

"We should get the rat out soon," she says.

"She's not a rat, she's a hamster," I say.

"Rat, hamster, rodent," says Gemma, "Holly is a rodent. Right. What plan do you have, given they've closed all the windows, including the one you normally go through?"

"How do you know which window I go through?"

"Because I watch you from the window in the female human's bedroom," Gemma replies with refreshing honesty and no noticeable sneer.

"We're stuck," I say. "Poor Holly, I feel so guilty leaving her behind."

"Don't be sorry, Frederick," says Gemma, "there's only one thing to do. You say this Egypt place is on the first floor and you get there via the stairs at the back?"

"Yes, Gemma, that's right."

"In that case, Freddie, we do our impression of Otto Skorzeny in World War II, by that I am referring to his daring rescue of Benito Mussolini from confinement at Campo Imperatore in the Abruzzi mountains where Marshal Pietro Badoglio had imprisoned him. I'm sure you're familiar with this rescue."

"No, no, I'm not," I say.

The crows shake their heads.

"Basically, Frederick, we go through the front doors – our combined weight should be enough to operate the pressure pads if we jump in the same place at the same time – and then run to the back, go up the stairs, get the rodent and return via the same route. Our advantage is our air cover with our crow friends here, who can dive bomb anyone who hinders our progress to the doors of the library. They are nature's equivalent of the Stuka."

"We are, you're right there," says Reg. "Should we get the park crows too, Stan, Sid, and Seb?"

"The more diversions the merrier," says Gemma.

"I'll get them," says Ron and flies over to the park.

"How will we get Holly out of the library?" I ask.

"Well, we need to appear to be doing the library a favour, so I'm going to carry her out of the library in my mouth, as though I'm ridding the library of a rodent problem. The humans will approve because it means they don't have to do anything, and that always makes them happy. Ah, reinforcements are arriving."

A small flock of crows land nearby, looking a little nervously at Gemma.

"This should be more than enough," says Gemma, "so we should go now on our rescue mission, because the longer we leave it the more worried the rodent will become."

"OK, I'll go first, I know the way," I say, and scamper away, closely followed by Gemma. The crows hover above us, providing air cover and bomb anything that appears to be in the way. When we arrive at the doors, the crows land on the telephone lines overlooking the front door.

"The pressure pad is here, Freddie," says Gemma, "3,2,1 jump."

We land together and the door whooshes open.

"Now run," says Gemma, and we sprint to the back of the library and although we hear gasps and comments of, "More cats?" we are up the stairs before people can really move.

"Egypt is over here," I say, "and I hope Holly has stayed put."

We jump onto the shelf, and I spy Holly.

"Holly, we should go. Gemma will carry you," I say.

"Gemma? Really?" says Holly. "Where is she?"

"Here," says Gemma. "Hello, rodent, don't worry, I will make this look good."

Gemma grabs Holly round the middle and we exit the way we came, with Holly squealing as we head towards the exit.

"The cat's got a rat," says someone. "Where did the cats come from?" says another. "Never mind that, where did the rat come from?" says a third.

"The pressure pad's here," I say, and we jump on it together and the doors open. The Stukas arrive and clear a path for us as we run around the fence and jump over the gate.

Gemma places Holly on the grass and takes a few deep breaths.

"Are you alright, Holly?" I ask.

"I am, actually," says Holly, "that was quite exciting. Thank you, Gemma for not using your teeth."

"You are welcome," says Gemma, "and thank you for the air cover, ladies and gents of the crow force, I saw you scored one or two direct hits on the gardener and the woman with the dog."

"Which woman with the dog?" I ask.

"The one who comes to our house for a drink or six," says Gemma. "She was videoing, but Abigail scored a direct hit on her phone, so that's the end of that video."

"That's an excellent shot, Abigail," I say.

"That's practice for you, Freddie," says Abigail. "I usually aim at the dog when she's in the park."

Everyone in the group falls about laughing as the dog is a Dalmatian puppy.

"So, what were you doing in the library?" asks Gemma.

"We were borrowing some cards that show squirrels and knives, so we can show them to the humans and then they'll shave Rufus's tail, so he'll be able to jump further on the slide in the park."

"Really...and you reckon the humans will understand this?" asks Gemma.

"Well, they're intelligent, aren't they?" I reply.

The crows are looking at Gemma with respect.

"Yes, we'll see about that. They're more likely to butcher poor Rufus and eat him at a barbecue. No offence, Rufus, but humans can be barbaric sometimes."

"I don't want that," says Rufus, "that's not part of the plan."

"No, it wouldn't be," says Gemma, "but there is a pair of scissors in the kitchen drawer, Freddie, so we could use those to suggest the humans trim the squirrel's tail. They don't normally cut up meat using scissors."

"That sounds much better," says Rufus, "but how will they know to trim the tail rather than cut the whole thing off?"

"Well, we'll have to show them a shaver too," says Gemma, "to give them the idea of shaving the tail rather than cutting it off, as you can't cut anything off, or sever anything, with a razor."

"That's good thinking, Gemma," I say, "but when would the best time be to do this?"

"Well, Freddie, there's no time like the present, is there,

you know, live in the moment like a Buddhist cat should, so I would suggest when they come home, assuming Mr. Rufus Squirrel here is available for a tail trimming."

"I'm ready to do it," says Rufus, "because if we trim today, I can go on the slide tomorrow and learn to fly further. I have to get the technique right and that might take a few days of practice."

"We need the picture of the squirrel, the picture of the knife, the actual scissors, and the razor together in one place along with the squirrel and ourselves, Freddie," says Gemma, "and then perhaps the humans might understand. He's squeamish so she might end up doing it, although we might have to observe if she uses the razor as he's the one who shaves daily and has a steady hand."

"It's complicated being a human," says Rob, "having to shave and brush their teeth in certain parts of their house and only being allowed to go to the toilet in a certain room. A lot of formality regarding their body, whereas we have complete freedom, no combing, no shaving, no brushing, no cutting."

"We're covered in fur," says Gemma, "so we have a lot of washing, at least the females do, male cats not so much, eh, Freddie?"

"I do some washing," I say, "but most of the time I'm busy doing other things, so I don't have time. Anyway, should we get the scissors and the razor, and where do we present them to the humans?"

"I'll get the scissors from the drawer. I can paw it open," says Gemma, "and bring them round to the front door on the outside. The humans won't want the squirrel inside the house.

No offence meant, Rufus, so if they trim anywhere it will be outside, so we should try to intercept them before they go inside the house. We'll need the book and the picture of the squirrel. I'd better hurry because they might be home soon." Gemma heads back to the kitchen window and I go to get the book from under the stairs, along with the cards. Hopefully, the humans, or one of them at least, will understand what we want them to help us with.

I scamper to the front door and place the items in front of it. I open the book at the page S for Squirrel so that the humans will see this first. The card of the pirate looks out of place.

As Gemma returns with the scissors, Jacqueline lands and says that the male human is walking back along the street and will be here in a minute.

"I won't have time to get the razor. We should stand either side of the door," says Gemma, "so he can see the pictures and then if he says squirrel then Rufus should appear, which will emphasise the point."

"That sounds good to me," says Rufus. "I will keep out of sight until he goes up the steps."

"And I will keep out of sight full stop," says Holly, "as I'm sure he will recognise me."

"We'll hang around the garden," says Reg, "just in case any help is needed."

"Sounds good," I say. "Here he comes now. He'll probably wonder why we're outside and not inside."

The male human comes through the garden gate and stops when he sees his two cats sitting outside their own front door.

"Hello, kitties," he says, "did we lock you out somehow this morning?"

Gemma and I miaow in unison as though it has been a hard day.

"There's a book open at the page S for squirrel and a picture of a knife and a pair of scissors and a picture of a pirate. What's going on, kitties, those are our scissors. How did you get them outside?"

Gemma curls her lip slightly. But instead of sneering, she pats the scissors with her paw, and I point at the tail of the squirrel with my left-front paw. Rufus also takes a couple of steps to come into sight.

"It's alright, Rufus," I say, "he's not going to hurt you."

"No, I know. He threw me a couple of nuts yesterday, which was very kind," says Rufus, rearranging himself so his tail becomes more prominently displayed.

"Wait, you want me to use the scissors on the squirrel?" says John.

Gemma miaows and I show the tail of the squirrel in the book.

"He's got something on his tail, and you want me to cut the fur on his tail?"

Both Gemma and I miaow in unison. Rufus looks pleased.

"And where does the pirate come in? Do I have to dress up as a pirate or do we have to perform this ceremony on board a galleon?"

I point at the sword of the pirate and then at the scissors.

"I see, so it's emphasising something sharp is required to trim the squirrel's tail?"

Gemma and I miaow again in unison.

"Well, I can't say I've done this before," says John, "I'll need some gloves from just inside the door," and he points at the gloves and then mimes putting them on.

"What's he doing?" says Rufus.

"He's going to put some hand coverings on," I say, "there's nothing to worry about."

"But my tail's clean," says Rufus, "I dip it in a puddle once a week and rub it thoroughly."

"He's doing it to protect you from human germs," says Gemma, "we wouldn't want you to catch anything nasty."

We stand aside as John moves the book and card, fumbles with the key before unlocking the door and goes inside. He returns wearing some gloves and picks up the scissors.

"Where's the squirrel?" he says.

Rufus is brave and places his tail towards the human.

"OK, I'm just going to examine the tail," he says and gently takes the tail in his hand. "It's almost all fur, well there's a surprise. OK, I will snip away the fur gradually until there's not much left. There seems to be some knotting of the fur in places, but we'll get rid of that." John snips a few times and the amount of fur on the step increases. He runs his hand down the tail and then cuts a bit more off. After about 5 minutes, he has reduced the tail in size by about 80%.

"Is this enough?" he enquires.

Rufus swishes his tail around and asks the crows what they think.

"It looks a lot better," says Reg, "you should fly further from the slide."

Rufus nods.

"You'll be a lot more aerodynamic," says Abigail, "with a lot less wind resistance."

"That's good to know," says Rufus. "I reckon that's enough trimming. Can you indicate that please, Freddie?"

"I will try," I say, and put my paw on the scissors in John's hand.

"I understand, I'll stop now," says John. "Thank you, kitties, and thank you, squirrel for staying still all that time."

Gemma and I miaow our thanks. Rufus wiggles his tail by way of thanks, although he might have been gauging its newly gained aerodynamic qualities.

John goes inside and puts the scissors in a jar. He places the squirrel hair in the compost bin and then picks up the book and the cards and examines them.

"What have you been up to?" he says. "These are the property of the library. Have they enrolled you kitties in the library? Shall I take them back?" He points at the book and cards and then indicates the library.

I miaow. This is a good thing, as this will cause less suspicion than if I trot into the library and leave the book and cards on the counter.

He heads through the gate.

"Well, that seemed to go well," says Gemma, "we seem to have achieved what we intended."

"I can't wait to go over to the park tomorrow," says Rufus, "and see how much further I can go off the slide."

"You should adopt a streamlined pose, not fly off the end with all four paws splayed out," I say. "You should stretch your front paws ahead of you and push your back paws behind you, so you have less of you hitting the wind."

"I see, I will have to practice," says Rufus, "I'll ponder it overnight."

"We're going to leave," says Seb, "we'll see you tomorrow by the sounds of it." The crows take off and give us a quick fly-by before heading over to the park. We watch them go.

"Well, that was fun," says Gemma. "I'm going inside to have a sleep before dinner." With that, she jumps onto the roof.

All this time, Holly had kept out of sight, because she knew John would recognise her. Now, she gives a polite cough and asks whether I can give her a lift back to her house, which I do before returning to the front door. I wait until the male human appears.

"Well, well, Frederick, what have you kitties been up to?" he says. "The librarians are all talking about two cats who ran into the library and then ran out again carrying a fully grown rat. One librarian was also crying because now she believes a phantom squirrel haunts the library, but I wonder whether there is a connection between the two events, as Holly the hamster is now running in her wheel over there whereas previously she wasn't even in her cage, and I've trimmed the very bushy tail of a squirrel?"

I stare at him with a far-away look in my eye and try to act innocent as he lets me in through the front door. I go under the sofa and fall asleep, content the day has been a success.

Chapter 13

Today

I DON'T HAVE ANY DREAMS overnight as the previous today had been a bit like a dream especially with a human trimming a squirrel's tail at the polite request of two cats and a flock of crows watching, plus a hamster hiding as she didn't wish to be recognised. Today is the moment of truth for the super squirrel who lives in the tree in the garden. Can he jump a foot further from the slide? Well, I hope so, because I can't think of another way to make him more streamlined, and he will be so disconsolate if he doesn't jump further – all that tail trimming for nothing. I cross my claws for him but then realise all the good karma we'd built up the previous day will help us today. I do a little meditation and feel my breathing and imagine myself sitting on the bench in the park, a small step-up from the molehill I used as inspiration last time, but it's an increase in height and that's a good thing, I'll make it to the mountaintop, eventually.

After completing my morning routine, I am relieved to see the kitchen window is still open; I am half expecting it to be closed and our trips outside curtailed. The humans are good people. The gap is narrower than the previous day, so Gemma may not squeeze through. I arrive at the base of the tree to see Rufus heading down towards me, more slowly than normal.

"Is everything alright, Rufus?" I ask.

"Oh yes," replies Rufus brandishing his tail. "Look at this, see how much thinner it is? Your male human did a wonderful cut on my tail, it's just that I have to be careful when I'm balancing because it's not as bushy as it was and so I need to rearrange my load slightly when moving to make sure I don't tip over."

"Right," I say, "redistributing the load is important, so you are balanced. Are you looking forward to the slide?"

"Oh yes," says the squirrel, "I'm really motivated to do well, but let's get across the road safely first, before thinking about the playground."

We approach the road and find a nice gap and gallop across, looking both ways in case of errant drivers.

We meet the crows in the park who insist that Rufus do a twirl with his new style of tail.

"It looks good," says Stan, "very streamlined. Do you want to go to the slide right away? I should warn you that the woman with the phone is around, so she might start filming you."

"That's fine," says Rufus. "She's free to do as she pleases as long as she's not harming anyone."

"That's very magnanimous of you, Rufus," I say. "My humans will be worried if they see a video of me over here, but as long as she films you and shows them the film of you flying, we'll be alright."

"Are you not going to have a go?" asks Rufus.

"No, I want to help you go further than you have done before, that's the focal point of today," I reply.

"Thank you, Freddie," says Rufus, "you're a great friend."

With that, we follow the squirrel to the slide. I remember where Rufus had landed before and make a mark with my paw in the grass in the landing area. I wonder if the squirrel will remember, because I have an inkling he is hoping to fly halfway to the swings.

RUFUS CLIMBS UP THE STEPS and walks to the edge of the platform before jumping up in the air slightly and heading down the slide. As he reaches the bottom, he throws his front paws forwards, grits his teeth, and soars past his previous record by a good 8 inches or two-thirds of a body length. Unfortunately, he lands face down, but gets his paws in the way just in time to avoid getting grass in his mouth and up his nostrils.

"How was that?" says Jacqueline.

"It was wonderful, and there was less drag through the air, so I must have gone further," he replies, looking at me hopefully.

"Oh, you did," I say nodding encouragingly, "nearly a squirrel length more than before."

"Excellent," says Rufus. "I'll have another go and push off with my back paws rather than just sliding off and see if that makes me go further."

"Try going down the slide headfirst," says Reg, "and then all your momentum will be in one direction."

"Yes, that's a great idea," says Rufus. "It will seem like

I'm diving down the slide, but I will have to have courage, won't I, Freddie?"

"You will, Rufus, you can do it, but it will need some practice."

"I have to remember why I had my tail trimmed because that took more courage than this."

He heads up the steps and breathes hard before hurling himself down the slide and pushing off the bottom edge with his back paws. He lands 4 inches further than previously. The next time is 2 inches further still and the time after that 1 inch.

"Well, Rufus," I say, "we're tired out watching you, but you're becoming obsessive now, the next time will be half-an-inch more and not noticeably further, so perhaps you should stop."

"Yes, thank you, I should. I am winded because I landed on my stomach all the time, but my paws and front legs took some of the impact. If I do this again, I won't have so many acorns for breakfast as they would weigh me down a bit. I hadn't thought of that. I might need to lose a bit of weight, but I'll see how I am this afternoon when I'm back in my tree."

"We should sit on the bench at the top of the park," says Reg, "I was getting quite tired watching you fly, Rufus, you've certainly got the technique worked out now."

"That's good," says the squirrel, "but I wonder how much further I can realistically go. Anyway, I will think about it later."

"You went one-and-a-half squirrel lengths further than last time," says Rob. "Just remember that Rufus and be proud of your achievement."

"Yes, it's been quite the 2 days," says Rufus. "I've had a great time, but need to relax a bit, eat some nuts and acorns, and think of the future."

I nod and smile at Sid, who raises his eyebrows at me. I hadn't realised crows had eyebrows until Sid makes the gesture and I realise how much I miss in the world around me sometimes, that seeing is not observing and watching is not understanding.

"Was the woman filming me?" asks Rufus.

"She might have been," says Seb, "because she was pointing her phone camera at you the whole time, and you never know she may have discovered the zoom feature so she could gain close-ups of the world's longest-jumping squirrel in action."

I giggle and Rufus looks pleased with himself all over again, the fur on his face stretching slightly around his mouth, showing a squirrel smile.

"Where's Gemma?" asks Rob. "Is she not interested in Rufus's exploits?"

"She is," I reply, "but she's sleeping this morning as she was on the Internet most of the night, recounting our exploits from yesterday, particularly on the fora where animals provide tips on helping each other. Apparently it's mostly dogs looking for advice on anger management and how not to bark so much, which really means effective barking for beginners."

"Well, the dogs in this park could do with going on that course," says Rob. "They bark at the drop of a leaf."

"Yes, and the smaller they are the more they bark,"

continues Abigail, "as though they're trying to make up for their lack of stature."

"That's right," I say, "it's making them feel important about themselves, as though barking makes them bigger in their own minds."

"I see a woman with a phone heading towards us," says Rob. "Her angle of attack is slightly different this time, coming in at 9 o'clock."

"Oh yes, and it's the one who visits my humans. She's called Penny, and she likes white wine," I say, "so there's no need to hide this time, as the male human at least has worked out that the cats in his house go out and about."

"She's very intent on taking her video and ignoring her dog, who's wandering about in front of her," says Stan. "If she's not careful she's going to trip over her own dog."

"At least it's on a lead," says Rufus. "You know, I've often wondered whether dogs would respond to having a squirrel as a jockey, a bit like humans and horses, whether there'd be any empathy between them."

"It would be more like bull riding," says Reg, "the dog would want you off its back as soon as possible and might try to roll around on the floor to achieve that. I know bulls don't do that, roll around I mean, but you'd not do much riding."

"It'd be fun to try," says Rufus. "I think I'll try it, when the dog's not expecting it."

"It won't be expecting to have a squirrel on its back ever," says Jacqueline, "but it has a collar and you've got strong front legs, so you could grip it tightly around the collar so that it has something to think about other than rolling about."

"That might be cruel to the dog," I say. "We shouldn't cause the dog any suffering, really we shouldn't."

There is a shriek, and Penny is on the floor, clutching her ankle while her dog whines. Penny's phone lies on the ground at the bottom of the slight slope where she'd overbalanced. Her foot had landed in a divot, and she wasn't concentrating properly and turned her ankle over.

"Rufus, no!" I say, but it is too late. Rufus sprints over to the dog and jumps on its back, gripping its collar and encouraging it to run.

I jump off the bench and get the phone. I grip it in my mouth and place it near Penny. Ron, Reg, and Rob walk over to the phone and look at the screen. Penny shouts, but the crows ignore her.

"We should dial the human emergency services," says Reg.

"Right, these are touch-sensitive screens," says Rob, "so touching with the beak should be enough."

Ron touches the green phone symbol, and a numeric keyboard appears.

"These keyboards are so small," says Ron. "Abigail, can you come and dial the number. You have a very delicate beak."

"This isn't happening," says Penny, "I need to get the phone."

Abigail comes over and taps at the keyboard three times. The number appears and the phone rings out.

"Ambulance, police, or fire," says the voice.

"Ambulance," screams Penny, "I've wrenched my ankle, I

~ 236 ~

can't move, I'm at the top end of the West Park, surrounded by crows and a cat and my dog's being ridden by an insane squirrel who's just been playing on a slide."

"And what's your name, madam?" says the voice.

"Penny, Penny Jones, but I'm the only one surrounded by animals, so I shouldn't be difficult to spot."

"Yes, madam, I will dispatch an ambulance right away, and I would like to remind you it is an offence to waste our time. The ambulance will be with you shortly. Maybe dial the Society for the Prevention of Cruelty to Animals regarding the creatures if they're a nuisance."

"And now we wait," I say, pushing the phone closer to Penny, so that she will be comforted by its presence in her hand, a feeling that seems to make humans happy, judging by the smiles on their faces when they're walking along with the phone out in front of them, like a guide dog without there being an actual dog there.

"Yee ha," says Rufus, as he comes by riding on the dog's back, with his rear legs gripping its flanks. He presses his legs together when he reckons the dog is flagging in its efforts.

"That squirrel is vicious," says Penny, "leave my Duchess alone, squirrel, you'll tire her out."

A minute or two later we hear the siren and retire to the bench to see what will happen next.

"Rufus, bring the dog back," shouts Seb. "The ambulance is nearly here. The dog will have to go to the hospital with its owner."

"Let's guide him back here," says Stan. "He's obviously become fixated on riding the dog into the ground." Stan, Sid, and Seb take off and head towards Rufus, who now seems to be hanging on for dear life and not enjoying the ride any longer.

"Rufus, jump off," I say as the dog hurtles past the bench.

"Caaaaaaannnn't," says Rufus, "goinggggggggggggg toooo faaaaast."

Eventually, Sid and Stan fly close to the dog's head and keep her turning, so she runs in ever decreasing circles until she stops and falls onto the ground with her tongue lolling out.

Seb grabs Rufus, who seems dizzy, and leads him to the bench where he rests against one of the metal supports.

"Over here," shouts Penny, as the medical team gets out of the ambulance and scan the park. She waves her hands around and one person points and sprints over to her as the other unpacks a stretcher on wheels.

"Which ankle is it?" asks the attendant.

"It's the left one," Penny replies, "I tripped over myself when I was filming those animals on the bench there," she points, "and my foot must have got caught in a divot or something."

"I will wiggle it around gently," says the attendant, "there may well be some pain. Is that your dog over there, the one that's whimpering on its side?"

"Owwww, yes, owwwch, the squirrel was forcing my Duchess to run around with it on her back, ayyow."

"Really, that squirrel over there that looks dizzy and is resting against the bench?"

"Yes, that's the one. It's in cahoots with that cat and the crows."

"They are admiring the view. The cat seems to be in meditation, it looks very peaceful."

"What have we here?" says the other attendant arriving with her stretcher. "And what's wrong with the dog, it sounds unhappy?"

"Apparently the squirrel was riding the dog around the park, abetted by the crows and the cat. Anyway, suspected torn ankle ligaments, we'll need a brace, and she should go to A and E." He radios the information into the hospital.

The two attendants place a large plastic boot on Penny's ankle and support her as she rises unsteadily and sits on the stretcher.

"Here's your phone," says the female attendant.

"I'll have to clean the screen," says Penny, "the crows tapped out the emergency number with their beaks."

The attendant looks at her sympathetically. "As you're sitting there, can we do a concussion test, you might have hit your head when you fell and not realised it. How many fingers am I holding up, dear?"

"Three," says Penny.

The other medic shines a light in Penny's eyes and asks her to follow their finger as they move it around. They feel Penny's head looking for any painful spots.

"You seem fine, dear," says the female attendant, "but crows don't normally phone the emergency services and squirrels don't act as jockeys and race dogs, so we might have to run some more tests just to be sure."

"You don't believe me, do you?" asks Penny. "You don't believe me, you think I'm making it up, look at my dog, look how tired she is, because that squirrel over there rode her into the ground."

"The squirrel looks exhausted – you know it looks like its tail's been cut, who'd have done that, it's cruel?"

"It's the cat that's the ringleader, I reckon," says Penny. "He may look all innocent, but he's got hidden depths that one. He goes into the library when he's not over here."

"Right," says the male attendant, "we should go. I'll place the dog under the stretcher, so she goes with you."

The man goes to pick up the dog and notices how she shrinks away from the bench when she sees the squirrel. He places the dog in a space at the foot of the stretcher and the attendants wheel Penny and Duchess away to the ambulance.

"Well, that was interesting," I say. "The attendants think Penny is delirious because she was describing what happened. How are you doing down there, Rufus?"

"I feel dizzy," replies the squirrel. "Racing around on that dog was not much fun after a while. I'm not doing that again."

"What possessed you to do it in the first place?" I ask. "You've never mentioned that as something you've always wanted to do."

"I know," says Rufus, "the truth is, Freddie, I'm a bit of a Jekyll and Hyde character at the moment. When I saw the dog looking lost, something took over and I wanted to ride around on its back, shouting like a cowboy. But now, I wonder what on Earth I was thinking of, what has that poor dog done to deserve that?"

"The dog had lots of exercise," says Abigail, "that's for sure. Learn to control yourself, Rufus. You're becoming obsessive about things, and anxious, first the flying and now the dog riding."

"Could it be a bad batch of acorns?" I ask.

"Well, it might be, because the last three I've eaten were from the cache that the evil squirrel Bertrand left behind, so maybe that wasn't his normal behaviour and the acorns made him behave in that horrible way."

"Toxic chemicals are disgusting," says Rob. "You should ditch those acorns, bury them and see if they produce trees. Trees that our great-great-grandchildren can perch in. That way at least those acorns will be useful."

"Yes, Rufus, plant those acorns in some soil, at least six feet apart and hopefully those trees will start growing soon," I say, "and you'll be doing the future a favour."

"It goes against my nature to bury acorns so that trees will grow, but I will do as you ask. How do you know about burying them six feet apart, Freddie?"

"I read it in a gardening book. It was about nurturing nature and I hoped that the information it contained would be useful one day and so it proved."

"It did indeed, young Freddie," says Sid, "you are a wise cat as normal."

"Anyway, Freddie, we should go," says Rufus. "We have that road to cross, and it's always a concern for me that it will be too busy. We should go."

"OK, Rufus," I say, "I will follow you as per usual."

Rufus appears none the worse for wear as we head over the grass accompanied by our crow friends who position themselves in the trees by the road. Rufus finds a gap for us and looks both ways. When there are no cars, we head over the road. At the same moment, the crows caw their approval of the gap.

"I'll plant those acorns," says Rufus. "Right now, there's some suitable soil in the front of your garden, I'll get them." He runs up the tree and is soon back clutching his food.

"You should plant them here," I say, "they'll get plenty of sun and rain in this strip of land."

"How deep?" asks Rufus.

"About half a front leg," I reply, "that should be ideal."

Rufus nods and sticks his front paw in the ground. He makes a small hole and places the acorn at the bottom of the hole. He then jumps twice along the soil and then plants the next acorn.

"You've done this before," I say. "You're a natural at this."

Rufus cackles and then makes two more hops to plant the final acorn. When that is done, he rubs his paws together and looks pleased.

"Well, Freddie, that's my good deed done for the day. My Dr Jekyll moment if you like. I will see you tomorrow." With that, he heads up the tree.

"See you tomorrow," I call after him. I hope he will be OK. It must be lonely up in his tree sometimes, especially if you're concerned about sudden changes in your mental state.

I trot back to the house and have a snack before settling down to read about Australia in the book *In a Sunburned Country*. Well, it sounds like a very scary place for a cat to be with spiders, snakes, crocodiles, and jellyfish that could kill me in an instant. Why would a small jellyfish that's only about a foot long pack enough of an electric shock to kill a human being and yet it only consumes tiny shrimps? I don't understand why a god would create this creature and on the other hand, I don't see why such a creature would evolve unless the jellyfish was being consumed in vast numbers by a larger animal, an animal that is no longer around, unless they've learned their lesson and don't go anywhere near the jellyfish. Who could blame them, though these animals would have to have a collective memory that was passed down through the generations, otherwise baby animals would repeat the mistake through the ages and die.

I also read a story about the desert rat kangaroo that out-sprinted horses for a distance of 12 miles non-stop in desert heat. This was many years ago and now the Australians have lost all these creatures, which seems rather careless. I doubt this is true though, because Australia is rather large, and these kangaroos have probably moved to a remote spot where humans don't go. I decide that the evolution of a lethal small jellyfish and a sprinting miniature kangaroo were suitable topics to meditate on and so I imagine myself sitting on top of a small hill cross-legged and thought of nothing, which leads me to fall asleep. Jellyfish and kangaroos sprouting from acorns fill my dreams and I wake up perturbed.

When we have our evening snack, Gemma seems happier than normal, so I ask her if anything is wrong.

"I enjoyed our trip to the library yesterday, Freddie. It was good to see those humans unable to process why two cats would invade their library in such a brazen manner. I was looking over there today and the vicar came again, presumably to get rid of the ghostly squirrel. They have closed the window you normally go through, so I think you might not be able to visit for a while, but don't worry, they'll soon drop their guard again. You can rely on that."

I tell Gemma about the book on Australia, and she says she'd like to read some of it, so we trot upstairs and hide beneath the sofa and read about Bill and the stromatolites he found in Australia. Stromatolites are special rock-like structures. They usually form in shallow water where cyanobacteria use water, carbon dioxide, and sunlight to create their food, and expel oxygen as a by-product. The real significance of stromatolites is that they are the earliest fossil evidence of life on Earth and almost certainly produced the oxygen that allowed all subsequent life forms to exist on the planet.

As we are reading, the doorbell rings. The female human answers.

There is a brief conversation outside before it heads indoors.

"...sorry to hear that. How long were you in hospital for?"

"About 3 hours. I've torn the ligaments in my ankle, which is why I have this protective boot on my foot for 2 weeks and I need crutches."

"Where did this happen? Come through to the kitchen and have a drink."

"Thank you, I will – it happened in the park when I was distracted by videoing your kitty cat sitting on a park bench with some crows..."

The conversation goes into the kitchen where the door closes on it.

"Did the squirrel fly further?" asks Gemma.

"He did, a good 8 inches further," I reply, "but I think that's enough to satisfy him for now. He calmed down for a few moments and then he went berserk and rode Penny's dog around the park and wore it out."

"Really? He spends too long on his own," replies Gemma, "but has she caught you on film over there?"

"Probably, because I did not evade detection."

"I'm not sure why she has this obsession, anyway the male human knows you go over to the park, so it will not be a problem."

"Do you think he knows?"

"Yes, you could tell by the way he looked at you, a mixture of admiration and worry, a bit like me when I see you go over there myself. I just hope you know what you're doing."

"Oh, thank you, Gemma, anyway we should continue reading. Bill's almost finished visiting Australia."

"You're right, Freddie, we should."

Gemma and I settle and continue to read together.

Made in the USA
Las Vegas, NV
22 October 2023

79471357R00142